THE THING WITH ZOLA

For my sonshine, Langalibalele.

THE THING WITH ZOLA

Zibu Sithole

MACMILLAN

First published in 2023
by Pan Macmillan South Africa
Private Bag X19
Northlands
Johannesburg
2116
www.panmacmillan.co.za

ISBN 978-1-77010-884-4
e-ISBN 978-1-77010-885-1

© 2023 Zibusisozethu Sithole

All rights reserved. No part of this publication may be reproduced, stored in or introduced into a retrieval system, or transmitted, in any form or by any means (electronic, mechanical, photocopying, recording or otherwise), without the prior written permission of the publisher. Any person who does any unauthorised act in relation to this publication may be liable to criminal prosecution and civil claims for damages.

This is a work of fiction. Any resemblance to actual events, places or persons, living or dead, is purely coincidental.

Editing by Nicola Rijsdijk
Proofreading by Katlego Tapala
Design and typesetting by Nyx Design
Cover design by Ayanda Phasha
Author photograph by Lana Wessels

Printed by **novus print**, a division of Novus Holdings

Even as the archer loves the arrow that flies, so too he loves the bow that remains constant in his hands.
– Nigerian proverb

Chapter 1

African time

Zola tapped lightly on her head – it was all she could do not to rip off her wig and dig her carefully manicured nails into her scalp. The heat was stifling, and the long strands of hair that floated across her face were annoying her.

Her interviewer was late.

Typical, she thought, her resentment growing with every minute. As if reacquainting herself with life back in South Africa wasn't enough, now the waiting in this oppressive heat. Her friends in Germany had always joked about 'African time', but it was even less funny in thirty-five degrees. It was just over an hour since she'd sat down at the table, and although technically she'd been early for the appointment – having given herself a cushion to mitigate taxi queues and traffic – in her books, Mbali Thabethe was now officially late.

Zola had only received one response after weeks of searching for vacancies across a range of industries, and then sending out her résumé and writing flowery covering letters: it was from Mbali Thabethe, who'd suggested they meet for an interview at an upmarket coffee shop. Zola had readily agreed. She wasn't fussy – all she wanted was a job, something to do while she planned her next move. But now Mbali was a no-show and Zola was seething.

In the hour that she'd been sitting here, the only people who'd noticed her were a couple of pot-bellied men who seemed to have nothing better to do than to leer at women in coffee shops all day. Five minutes earlier, an arrogant young charmer who must be all the rage where he's from had walked towards her table and smiled with recognition, his bald head gleaming and his muscled arms straining at the arms of a tailored suit. He'd even had the gall to pull up a chair and sit across from her. Creep.

Zola had looked him up and down, her nostrils flaring. It was beyond her. His shining white teeth, perfectly straight, would usually have impressed her, but his presumption at this critical moment in her life churned her stomach – the guy clearly had no idea who he was messing with. The twist of his lips as he started to speak was just the sign Zola needed to grab her bag and leave. With a long click of the tongue that left the roof of her mouth ringing – she'd actually forgotten she could do that – Zola had stalked away from the table and found the waitress to pay for her Coke.

'Great,' Zola mumbled now as she sashayed out of the coffee shop. Another wasted taxi trip, all in her favourite stilettos.

Tears burned behind her eyes and all she could think was that this wouldn't have happened in Germany. None of this had been part of her plan: the expired visa, lack of work permit, nothing more to study and every job-application rejection that had followed.

When Zola had first been accepted into the bursary scheme in Germany ten years ago, she'd been so excited. She'd carefully chosen her high-school subjects and even her extra-curricular activities and kept up her grades to make sure she'd get in. And now, it was over – she was out.

THE THING WITH ZOLA

It had never even crossed her mind that she'd have to come home. She hadn't made any plans to leave Germany, and had even avoided visiting her family so that everyone could get used to the idea that she had a *new* home. And now here she was, hobbling towards the taxi rank like she'd never left Jozi.

Her German friends, her boyfriend, her favourite restaurant and the coffee shop she loved around the corner from her chic city apartment in Munich – all of it might as well be a fantasy. And her glowing recommendations and sterling distinctions seemed to be no help at all – in fact, she was convinced they were holding her back. She was overqualified, her dreams too big for this small place she occupied in the world, and she didn't know how to make herself any smaller.

She ground her teeth and cat-walked her way through the burning pain in her feet, her arches feeling as if they were about to snap. Still, she refused to walk barefoot with her heels in her hand – she may be down, but pattering barefoot through the streets of Rosebank was well beneath her.

The taxi ride home was a blur of disjointed thoughts. She'd sworn to herself that she would never end up back here, though she'd looked forward to a few impactful visits home – like, after getting her first high-paying job, she'd fly in and buy her mother a bigger, better house, fully furnished with all-new appliances, in a suburb where she wouldn't need to sweep the curb in front of her front door. She'd make another trip home to arrange a quick but glamorous wedding, and she'd come out again to introduce the family to her gorgeous new baby. Yes, she'd had her entire life planned – and with just one visa rejection, it had all fallen apart.

Now she was just like one of her many unemployed cousins, reduced to doing housework and chores. Just like that, her 'rich aunty' membership had been cancelled. From Aston Martin dreams to a rickety old taxi – as she transferred coins and crumpled notes over the shoulders of strangers, Zola pulled her head as far back as she could to avoid the passing bottoms of her fellow passengers as they reached their stops.

'How was the interview?' Nomsebenzi asked as soon as Zola walked through the door.

Zola threw herself onto her mother's lumpy sofa and kicked off her shoes. She heaved a sigh of relief – finally, her feet were free. With another deep breath, she prepared to rant.

'I don't know how women are going to find their place in the corporate world when we continue to undermine each other like this,' she huffed. 'She was a no-show, not even a phone call to let me know she wasn't coming.' Zola's voice rang with a practised twang, even in rage.

Used to her daughter's ravings, Nomsebenzi didn't respond. Whether she agreed with Zola or not would make no difference – she knew Zola would go on and on. Her voice would get louder as she riled herself up until she was too exhausted to continue, though she was never actually out of words. Zola was never short of words.

It wasn't so much that Nomsebenzi had nothing to say, just that she knew Zola wouldn't hear her. Not in her current mood. So Nomsebenzi just nodded her head, working her fingers around the potato she was diligently peeling. She had known from Zola's first cries that her daughter would be hard to satisfy, that the simple life she could offer on her cashier's salary would never be enough. Zola had always and would always want more.

And today she wanted more than to be stood up by her interviewer.

'I mean, who the hell does she think she is?' Zola spat, not pausing to let her mother get a word in. 'She's running a freakin' start-up, she doesn't even have a formal office yet, and she's already treating people like garbage!'

Droplets of sweat bubbled onto Zola's forehead and the hair that this morning had been so carefully arranged around her shoulders now poked at her neck, itching like a cheap scarf.

With practised precision, Zola took off her wig and threw it across the living room, through the open door of her bedroom and onto her bed.

'Mbali Thabethe can go to hell!' she shrieked, her twang finally failing her.

Zola's younger sister, Thobile, walked out of their shared bedroom, hiding a small smile.

'Mbali Thabethe?' she asked, scrolling through her phone. 'You were going to meet *the* Mbali Thabethe?'

Zola's nose flared as she glared at Thobile. She hadn't missed the supressed laughter in her voice.

'Sis' ... you know Mbali is a *man*, right?' Thobile said passing Zola her battered phone.

Through the cracked screen, Zola recognised the grin of the man she had left smiling expectantly at the coffee shop.

Mbali Thabethe *had* arrived for their meeting. And he'd been her only hope, the only response she'd received after weeks of fruitless job-hunting.

'Shit,' Zola whispered.

Chapter 2

Reality check

'What kind of man is named Mbali?' Zola croaked. The more she stared at the picture of Mbali on Thobile's phone, the more his smile taunted her. The curl of his lips seemed to rise in a sinister smirk, payback for her snooty attitude when he had arrived, perfectly on time and as agreed, for her interview.

Her embarrassment rose like a hot flush.

'Seriously?' Thobile snatched back her phone. 'This is *his* fault?'

Zola felt her mouth go dry; her tongue felt too big. The room grew smaller, hotter. Thinking of how she had left the coffee shop, she wished her body would drop into the ground and be swallowed whole.

'And now?' Thobile giggled, sitting down next to her sister and zooming in on the smiling Mbali on her phone. 'Is he that hot in real life?'

Zola's vision was blurred with tears and her chest tightened. How could she have been so stupid?

'Get her water,' Nomsebenzi told Thobile, and hurried to Zola's side to fan her furiously with the thin cutting board she'd been using.

It wasn't the cold air or her mother's muttering that snapped Zola back. It was the smell of onions – everything her mother cooked started off with onions fried in oil that was too hot, and was followed by a cube of beef stock. It didn't matter if she was cooking cabbage or chicken or fish – everything Nomsebenzi cooked tasted the same to Zola, flavoured with her mother's tired choices. The too-familiar smell would mark every evening of her life if she didn't fix this.

'He was there,' Zola croaked, the swirling confidence of her rant evaporated.

'And what? He just ignored you? He probably just didn't see you,' Thobile offered, handing Zola a cold glass of water. 'Just send an email and clear it up.'

'Nooooooo …' Zola moaned, gulping down the water so quickly she almost choked. 'I was expecting a woman so I …' The memory of Mbali's face came back clearly, his Colgate smile, the smell of his cologne wafting across the table to her, as bile rose in her throat.

'She did *what*?' Mthunzi laughed into his drink.

Mbali ran his hand over the smooth skin of his scalp and called her face to memory. He was still intrigued by the woman who'd sat across from him so indignantly before she'd just upped and left. That was the last thing he'd expected.

'I'm telling you, bro – she just called me a creep and headed out.' Mbali shrugged. 'I don't know, man. I was literally maybe two minutes late, but she obviously took it personally.'

Zola's CV was still open on his laptop as he snapped it closed and cleared his desk. His office was a small, musty room in one of the many office buildings his father owned. It was an insult to the suave persona he put out on social media, but it was a start – a start he had hoped to make along with one overqualified Germain-trained logistician and his long-time friend Mthunzi, who'd been his shadow since they were in primary school.

'I don't like that look, dude. I know how crazy brings out the stupid in you. She's a lost cause,' Mthunzi pleaded, taking another swig of his whisky. 'Besides, can you imagine having to share this tiny space with her? I don't think so.'

Mbali packed up, methodically checking some files off a list before sliding each one into his briefcase. Without looking up, he sighed. 'You know, I don't like the look of you drinking in here. This is a place of work, man. No one will take us seriously if it smells of booze every morning.'

'Sorry, m'fethu.' Mischief brimmed in Mthunzi's eyes – while he was clearly past feeling shame, he was not past pretending to be sorry. 'I know you're trying to build some serious image here, but you also can't go around stalking every crazy chick you meet just because they had the wisdom to reject you.'

'You, my friend, need to stop calling women crazy – that never ends well. And besides, I just wanted to offer her a job, not marry her,' Mbali said thoughtfully.

When Mbali had first seen Zola's CV, he knew he'd struck gold. All the other applicants boasted years of experience and connections – which meant he couldn't mould them into what he needed. He needed someone specific for this Dubai tender. There was nothing that special about transporting building equipment from one place to another – he knew he could do that – but he'd wanted to impress his father with a certain level of professionalism and flair.

Zola was definitely impressive. And she definitely had flair. Maybe too much, he thought sadly. He'd really hoped she'd come onboard with them, but now he didn't know what to think.

As usual, Mthunzi just didn't get it. Like the expensive whisky he preferred, Mthunzi was an acquired taste. While Mbali struggled to get out of his father's looming shadow, Mthunzi was only too happy to do as little work as possible. They both knew that without Mbali's father's generous stipend at the end of every month, Mthunzi would be a bum.

Mbali slid the whisky bottle out of Mthunzi's reach and sat on the edge of his desk in its place. 'Maybe having an actual professional in here would make this feel more like an office and less like a bar,' he said seriously. 'Look, man, we need to make good on this Dubai pitch. This deal could really put us on the map.'

Mthunzi stared at him blankly. 'Come on, bra, your dad's giving this to us on a silver platter. It's as good as done. Dubai, here we come!' he shouted, and stumbled to his feet.

'Mthunzi, I'm serious,' Mbali pressed. 'This is not a holiday. We need to make this work. My dad is getting us through the door, but we need to make this one happen on our own.'

'It's a done deal, bro – your dad said as much. We just need to show face and have a good time. I don't get why you always have to look for the hardest way to do things when we both know we're set for life.' Mthunzi waddled clumsily out of the office, his jacket dragging behind him.

Mbali watched him leave.

The trip to Dubai had been organised and paid for by Mbali's father, who had already put in a word for his son and Mthunzi. But Mbali still wanted to make an impression – and not the one Mthunzi seemed determined to make. The thing was, Mbali knew that things were easy for him, they always had been, and it bugged him. There was so much going on around him, so much opportunity, but he'd never done things on his own terms. And he wasn't stupid – he knew all that could change, all those opportunities could disappear.

If he ever disagreed with his dad, they definitely would.

Zola sat on her bed squinting into the screen of her laptop. How was she going to explain to a prospective employer that she'd thought Mbali was a woman without admitting that she hadn't even done a web search on the person who'd agreed to interview her? Her CV said she was diligent, paid close attention to detail and was personable and easy to work with. Her regrettably short encounter with Mbali said otherwise.

'Zola? Not sleeping tonight?' her mother asked stepping into her room and handing her a hot cup of tea.

Without looking up from her screen, Zola took the tea and put it on the nightstand that stood between her and her sister's beds.

'I need to fix this, Mama. It's the only chance I've had in months – I can't just let it go. I can't be stuck here.'

'*Stuck* here,' Nomsebenzi repeated slowly, as if she was unsure what the words meant.

Zola looked at her mother for the first time since she'd come into the room. She knew her mother was hurt. Nomsebenzi was hurt every time Zola mentioned leaving or wanting something better than the life she'd lived before she'd been able to do anything about it.

It wasn't intended, but Zola's ambitions appeared to her mother like scorn for the life she had done her very best to provide. Although Zola now knew they fell well below the middle class, Nomsebenzi had always made sure her girls didn't feel poor. They hadn't had to worry about having enough food or clothes, and they had always enjoyed life's simple pleasures. Nomsebenzi had done whatever was needed to provide for her children – she'd sacrificed her pride and borrowed money, deprived herself of clothes, furniture and simple conveniences like taking a taxi, instead walking for half an hour.

'You know, Zola, you don't know how lucky you are. The life and the home you take for granted is something others may dream about,' Nomsebenzi said, unable to hide her hurt.

'I don't take it for granted, Mama, but it isn't a sin to want better,' Zola argued.

Zola hadn't recognised her mother's sacrifices until she was older and had secretly started making sacrifices of her own. Zola had always wanted better – not just for herself, but for her mother too.

'You know what I mean,' Zola said casually. 'I just need this job.' She stared at the screen and deleted the email she had crafted.

Just then, as if he knew she needed the distraction, Zola's phone rang. Günter.

'I miss falling asleep next to you,' he said in his sleepy German drawl as soon as Zola answered.

Zola looked apologetically at her mom. Nomsebenzi knowing about Zola's boyfriend across the ocean was one thing; being in on their pillow talk was another thing completely.

'Don't stay up too late,' Nomsebenzi whispered as she walked out, deliberately leaving the door open.

Chapter 3

Waking up with Günter

The downy hair on Günter's body tickled Zola's face, his musky smell filled her nostrils and she snuggled closer to him, tucking the sheets closer under her chin. The apartment was always just a little too cold, but it was an excuse to cuddle closer, to feel his chest rising and falling with every breath.

Through a foggy sleep, Zola was dimly aware of noise around her. It was never noisy at her and Günter's place. Never in the six years that they'd lived together had she ever been woken by a knock on the door or the sound of neighbours moving about. They had seldom had anyone stay over and certainly no one who would be muttering so close in isiZulu ...

Slowly, Zola woke up to her reality and peeked out from under the covers. She was in bed, alone. In her mother's house in Vosloorus. And Günter wasn't there.

'Really now, if you aren't talking to your man all night, you're moaning and groaning in your sleep. How do you expect me to get a good night's rest?' Thobile complained, struggling groggily to get her school jersey over her head without messing up her carefully laid edges.

It wasn't a good morning and Zola already knew it wouldn't be a good day. Her conversation with Günter the night before had been filled with longing and impatience, a chilling foreboding that a relationship across two continents might not work. Since the day they'd met, they'd never been further than a bus ride from each other. Neither of them was prepared for the long-distance relationship that had been so unexpectedly thrust upon them.

Zola had met Günter during her first week in Germany. Her classes hadn't started yet and she'd been feeling like she'd made a huge mistake.

'Eh?' the building manager had grimaced as Zola imitated the hissing sound the fridge in her room had been making. Her descriptions had grown more and more animated as her desperation grew, but she'd only managed to confuse the elderly woman, who apparently didn't speak a word of English.

'Hssss!' Günter had hissed back at her as he walked passed the two mystified women. He was tall, large and as thickly set as the trunk of an old tree – a Germanic gym bro with generic good looks. His body had said he was into sports, hiking. His crumpled plaid shirt over tight-fitting jeans suggested that he probably liked camping. This had instantly irritated Zola, but as far as the fridge was concerned, he had been her only hope. She'd looked up at him and felt tears running down her cheeks. He'd softened, his lips curling in a sympathetic smile.

'She doesn't speak English,' he'd said walking two steps closer to Zola.

'I've noticed,' Zola had mumbled, roughly wiping her tears with the back of her hand.

He'd stood too close to her but she'd needed him so she'd stood there, his arm lightly grazing hers, and tried once more to explain the fridge situation.

'The. Fridge. In. My. Room. Is. Hissing,' Zola said slowly. 'I. Can't. Sleep.'

Günter nodded with every slowly pronounced word. Then he cleared his throat and mimicked Zola's patronising tone right back at her: 'She. Does. Not. Speak. English.'

His unblinkingly blue eyes had fixed on her. Even though he smiled, she could not bring herself to meet his gaze, so she stared at his lips as they forced out words spoken with a rough nasal accent.

'But I can hear you just fine and, most importantly, I can translate.' Günter smiled before rattling off something in German.

It was Zola's turn to nod, even though she had no idea what he was saying, and suspected it was a lot more than she had told him.

'Oh,' the building manager said before rattling off her own list of what sounded like complaints, and walking away.

At which point Günter also started to walk away.

'Wait,' Zola called, trotting behind him and trying to catch up to his long quick strides. 'What did she say?'

Günter turned and stopped abruptly, his brows furrowed. 'Do you want to have breakfast with me?' he asked.

'*Excuse* me?' Clearly things were very different in Germany than they were at home.

'Breakfast,' Günter said, motioning to eat with his hands.

'What did she say?' Zola repeated.

Günter smiled again and Zola felt her heart leap involuntarily as her lips spread in a toothy smile.

'You're not getting a new fridge. No one will be coming to fix the fridge in your room for a very long time,' he chuckled, then casually offered his arm, as if fully expecting her to hook hers around it. 'So, breakfast then?'

Zola had been halfway through her breakfast before Günter had actually introduced himself: he was preparing for his third first year as a student. He had started to study Law, then Art History and was now taking a casual stab at a degree in Philosophy.

Günter then stared in awe as Zola explained the very detailed plan she'd had for as long as she could remember: she was going to become an industrial engineer and travel through Europe working and studying and making an obscene amount of money before she settled down, got married and had two children by the time she was thirty-five. She had seventeen years to do it – and although that sounded like a long time, for all the things she wanted to do, it wasn't. There was no room for guessing or mistakes.

'Wow,' Günter said too loudly, leaning back in his chair and stretching his long arms over his head. 'And what happens when these big, big plans of yours don't work out exactly the way you want them to?'

Their breakfast had long been finished. Their plates had been cleared and an impatient waitress had already asked them three times if they needed anything else. Günter didn't seem to care, and Zola hadn't had anyone to talk to since she'd been dropped off at the student housing complex a few days earlier.

'It *has* to work out,' Zola sighed, forcing herself to ward off the stench of desperation that she was sure clung to her. 'It *will* work out, you'll see,' she said with more confidence this time.

Rubbing sleep from her eyes, Zola remembered how everything had just fallen into place that morning: meeting Günter, a man she wouldn't ordinarily have looked twice at. And they had fallen into a comfortable but unlikely love.

Of course her plans had changed – they'd had to. As things had turned out, she'd never travelled across Europe – either to study or to work. She'd found one way after another to stay in Germany with Günter.

Until she had exhausted them all.

Finding herself crying on a red-eye flight back home had been like waking from a decade-long dream.

'I hope you aren't bringing home a tiny stranger,' Aunt Mina had laughed, greeting her at the airport.

Zola didn't think it was funny, and she appreciated the comments about her weight gain even less.

'You clearly didn't miss home,' her aunt said, patting her on the bum. 'The Germans fed you well.'

Zola glared at her mother. She'd asked her not to bring her sister to the airport, but there Aunt Mina had been, as immoderate as ever, rubbing salt in all of Zola's old wounds.

That had been six months ago, and nothing much had changed until the botched interview with Mbali 'I-am-actually-a-man' Thabethe. Zola sighed, put her head under the covers and allowed herself another half hour of sleep.

Thobile had long left for school by the time Zola finally rolled out of bed and headed to the kitchen, hoping she now had the house to herself.

But no.

'The porridge is cold in the pot,' Nomsebenzi announced the minute Zola emerged from her room. 'Warm some up and get ready. Mina and Zozo are on their way already. We're going to Plaza to get some curtains.'

Zola had known this wouldn't be a good day – she just hadn't counted on it being so bad. A three-taxi ride to Plaza with her loud aunt gossiping about everyone around them and her cousin Zozo repeating the latest drama about her boyfriend, Thabo, was the last thing Zola needed.

'I'll stay home.' Zola scooped the congealed brown porridge into a bowl. 'I'm waiting for a response to my email,' she added quickly.

Nomsebenzi stared knowingly at Zola – she knew Zola could check her email on her phone from anywhere.

'I'm not saying this to be hurtful, but someone has to tell you this, Zola,' Nomsebenzi said seriously. 'Rather me than someone on the street.'

Zola could see her mother peeling off the kid gloves she'd been coddling her with since she'd returned from Germany. Reluctantly she sat down to her cold porridge with a side helping of Nomsebenzi's famed 'straight talk'.

'My girl, you have your nose so high in the air you can't even see what's in front of you,' Nomsebenzi said, turning her head up to the ceiling.

'Fine. I'll go to Plaza, Mama,' Zola said rolling her eyes.

Nomsebenzi shook her head and moved over to rinse dishes in the sink.

'It's this attitude you have; you don't think anyone here is on your level. That isn't going to get you anywhere,' Nomsebenzi continued, ignoring Zola's change of heart.

Zola sighed. The porridge felt like cold sludge in her mouth. 'What do you want me to say, Mama?'

'You think you're better than everyone. If you didn't, you wouldn't have been so rude to that man Mbali and maybe you'd have a job now.'

Not wanting to even witness Zola's reaction to her intentional delivery, Nomsebenzi disappeared into her room with perfect timing.

Zola's appetite left with her mother; she couldn't stomach another spoonful of her breakfast. It was one thing to know what her mother thought, but it still stung to hear her say it.

And Zola knew it was all her fault. Her attitude *was* the reason she'd missed out on the only job opportunity she'd had since she came home.

It was also the reason she hadn't been able to stay in Germany.

Chapter 4

Regret

If you asked on a good day, Zola would tell you she'd done everything to stay in Germany. But on the taxi ride to Johannesburg with her sweaty arm pressed tightly against her cousin Zozo's, she knew that wasn't completely true.

'You don't have to leave,' Günter had said softly as they'd walked back from the Ausländerbehörde.

Zola had received an email stating that her visa wouldn't be renewed, but somehow felt it was some mistake she could fix by talking to someone face to face at the immigration authority.

That wasn't how it had worked out. She wasn't sure how exactly, but she blamed Günter.

'Did you *hear* what the woman said?' Zola had whispered through clenched teeth. 'I have no visa so, no, I can't just stay. It's absolutely ridiculous!'

Günter had been downcast for the rest of the way home. Until he'd met Zola, he'd never taken anything seriously in his life – he'd never had to – and since that day their relationship had become his entire identity. He now didn't have any friends Zola didn't like, didn't wear clothes that Zola didn't approve of, and he had actually finished his degree, much to the shock of his parents. These days he had a stable job at the university, he was studying further, he had a plan for the future – all because of Zola. And it all fell apart without her.

He followed her into their apartment and looked around. Everything in it reminded him of her and even as she moodily banged the bathroom door behind her, he knew one thing: he didn't want her to leave.

'Marry me,' he stammered through the closed bathroom door.

Inside the small room, Zola was quiet. She couldn't move, even held her breath.

The silence in the apartment grew thick and heavy.

'Zola?'

Zola flushed the toilet and washed her hands, slowly lathering the soap under the running tap. Zola was a planner. She had already imagined every detail of her life, from her dream proposal to the inevitability of growing old alongside her soul mate.

This particular scenario had never occurred to her.

Knowing he was just a few centimetres on the other side of the closed door, she stood for a moment before opening it slowly, which gave Günter enough time to stand up and straighten out.

'Marry me?' Günter repeated as she came out.

Zola blinked. Seeing him say the words made it even less real to her. Her lips moved but no words emerged; her thoughts drifted in her head like fireflies, just out of reach.

'It just makes sense, Zola. We can get it done at the courts and then you could stay. I mean, it wouldn't even look suspicious – we could easily pass whatever tests they throw our way,' Günter said quickly.

Even as the words rolled out of his mouth, he knew it wasn't the right thing to say.

'A *visa* marriage?' Zola said slowly, her eyes filling with tears.

Günter took a deep breath and wondered if it was too late to take it back, say something more romantic.

'That's what you think of me?' Zola asked, her voice shaking. 'I'm some poor African you're helping out? My magnanimous white saviour saving me from my sad life back home?'

The blood drained from Günter's face. Surely she knew that wasn't how he felt about her? Not after all these years, not after he'd willingly dreamt Zola's own dreams alongside her?

Zola pushed past Günter and grabbed her handbag.

'I should have known this was what you were about! You and your posh family patting each other's backs every time you did even the smallest thing for me!' Droplets of spit flew from her mouth. 'Gold star for you for housing me all this time – God knows what would have become of me without you!'

'Zola, please! I don't understand why you're saying this. You *know* I love you,' Günter pleaded, his heart pounding in his chest.

'And aren't you the saint!'

Zola slammed the door behind her.

The memory of that conversation made Zola's body itch, even though in the end she'd put it down to the stress of having her life fall apart. In the weeks that followed, Günter had seemed tense and he hadn't asked her to marry him again.

'Thinking about your Italian stallion?' Zozo whispered now in the taxi, her eyes lit with a naughty glint.

Zola faked a smile. 'He's not Italian.'

'Whatever. You thinking about him, aren't you?' Zozo giggled. 'I know that smile, that's how I smile when I think of Thabo.' She bit her bottom lip suggestively.

Zola rolled her eyes. Zozo's stories never lacked any detail, and her graphic descriptions of Thabo had found a permanent place in Zola's mind. Now, at the mention of his name, a vivid image of Thabo walking nude across his room came to mind, the slow roll of his buttocks described by Zozo with salacious slurps of her tongue. Zola shuddered at the thought.

Her phone buzzed with a message alert. She pulled it out of her bag and scrolled through her emails, her hands shaking as she ran her fingers over the screen. It was just an email about something in her online shopping cart being on sale.

Zola's heart sank. She'd been hoping Mbali would reschedule her interview – the second chance she knew her mother had been praying for.

'Still waiting for your good-morning text from Günter?' Zozo asked smugly. 'Thabo sends me a message the moment he wakes up, then we talk on the phone on his way to work. I couldn't stand it if he didn't at least send a good-morning text.'

Zola turned away and looked out of the window at the people walking hurriedly through the busy streets. Everyone was in a rush here, even when they weren't.

'I think you should break up with him, Zola. I mean, what's the point? You deserve so much better, cuz,' Zozo said, worming her neck.

Zola nodded solemnly, hoping it would shut Zozo up. She wanted to be left to her misery, feel every sour thought until they reached their stop.

As soon as the taxi slowed down, scooting close enough to strangers to smell their breath, Zola moved towards the front, wrestled open the door and hopped down – straight into a slimy puddle of muddy water. She stifled a scream and stepped aside to allow Zozo, then her mother and then her aunt to step cautiously over the puddle. Then she slammed the taxi door so hard that it disconnected from its rails.

'And you'll put that door back,' the driver said without even turning to look at her, his calm instruction underpinned with menace.

Even after all this time, Zola hadn't forgotten the particular humiliation that came with breaking something on an already rickety taxi, the quiet stares of other passengers willing you to quickly get it right so they could get to their destinations, the silent impatience of a taxi driver who truly believes he has put you in your place.

With shaking hands, Zola tried to right the door until the driver eventually climbed out of his seat, glared at her and effortlessly put the door back on its rails.

'I can't wait until Thabo gets his car,' Zozo said, grimacing at the taxi as it finally drove off. 'Once Thabo gets a car, you and I will never need to see the inside of a taxi again, cuz.'

The women fell in line with the strangers on the crowded pavement, and followed Zozo as she set the pace for a fast walk through the gates of Plaza.

'Sure as fuck,' Zola muttered under her breath.

Chapter 5

The unexpected

By the end of the day, between Aunt Mina's constant jibes about how 'They don't have *this* in Germany' and Zozo's endless chatter about Thabo, Zola was exhausted.

She lay in bed staring at the ceiling, her mind blank. When Thobile came in from school, Zola still didn't get up, and she didn't even complain about the music that was soon blasting in their shared room.

'What's wrong with your daughter?' Thobile asked her mother as the two of them sat down to have dinner – Zola had stayed lying on her bed.

'You know her moods,' Nomsebenzi said, with some guilt. Maybe she'd been too hard on Zola. But her eldest daughter had always been precocious – she'd known what she wanted from the very beginning.

When she was a baby she'd refused the breast, and Nomsebenzi had felt rejected. Her daughter was fiercely independent and didn't even seem to need her. Her marriage to Zola's father had been cold, and when Zola was born she'd hoped she would finally get the warmth and love she needed.

She'd had to wait. It was only when Thobile was born that she got the closeness she'd so desperately wanted – a daughter who actually wanted to know what she thought. Of course, there had then been the childhood sibling rivalries to deal with, and more coldness and judgement from an adolescent Zola. And then she was gone.

For weeks after Zola had left for Germany, she had not called home. She hadn't let anyone know that she was safe, how she was doing or if she needed anything. Nomsebenzi had taken it personally and she still held a grudge. The truth is, when she'd snapped at Zola about looking down on everyone, she'd meant herself. She was convinced Zola hadn't bothered calling because even if she had needed something in Germany, there really wasn't anything Nomsebenzi could do for her. That feeling of helplessness crept up on her again – the same one she'd felt as she'd struggled to nurse her tiny but fierce newborn. She was keenly aware that she didn't have any connections or job offers lined up for Zola. She had failed to do what other parents could do for their children and it made her angry – not at Zola, but at herself. It pained her to see her feisty child so low.

'Just be gentle with your sister for now, okay?' Nomsebenzi pleaded with Thobile. 'She's going through a really tough time, and she doesn't deserve grief after how hard she's worked.'

Zola heard her mother through the open door of her bedroom and wished she could get up and run to her. She wanted to hug her mother tightly and feel the soft warm safety of her arms.

But she was exhausted. Tears fell from her eyes, down the sides of her face and pooled in the ridges of her ears as she drifted off into a dreamless sleep.

There was no telling how long she'd been sleeping when she woke up with a start.

The house was quiet and she could hear both her mother and Thobile's deep breathing. She reached for her phone to check the time and saw a new email had come in: a meeting request from Okuhle Msimanga, owner of an events-management company called Larger Than Life.

Okuhle's email was short and to the point: she was looking for a project manager and believed Zola could be it. And she wanted to meet first thing the next morning at her offices in Rosebank.

What could Okuhle possibly want from Zola, an industrial engineer? She knew next to nothing about events, and she wasn't a project manager. She also hadn't applied for a job at Larger Than Life.

It was a scam, Zola was sure. But she was now wide awake, so she typed in a few keywords to see what Google had to say on the matter. And the more she read about Larger Than Life, the more impressed she was, not only with the company but with Okuhle herself.

She didn't organise children's parties and low-budget weddings – she curated expos and conventions all over the world. It wasn't exactly her dream job, but Zola could already see herself growing and thriving alongside Okuhle, who wasn't even that much older than her.

A new dream, Zola decided, smiling to herself as she set her alarm and fell back to sleep. She would never admit it, but she somehow felt her changing luck might have something to do with her mother – Nomsebenzi had been burning incense and saying endless prayers.

By the time the sun rose and Zola's alarm went off, she was already sitting up in bed reading every interview Okuhle had ever done. Zola had watched her TV interviews too and scrolled through her social media. In a matter of hours, Zola had gone from not knowing who Okuhle was to becoming her biggest fan.

'Thobile, wake up,' Zola said, leaning over to switch off her alarm. 'Wake up or I'll get in the bathroom before you and you'll be late for school.'

'You're happy today,' Thobile observed with a growl.

Zola smiled to herself. 'I guess I am.' She threw open the curtains and unfastened the window. She took a deep breath of the fresh morning air and hit the first snag in her plans for the day: rain.

'I have an interview today,' Zola told Nomsebenzi as she bustled in to inspect Thobile's school uniform.

Their mother sighed deeply, wrapped her arms around Zola and squeezed her tightly. 'You're going to get this one, Zola – I can feel it.'

Unusually, Zola didn't shrug. She took in all her mother's warmth and started to figure out what to wear to her interview with Okuhle from Larger Than Life.

Mbali knitted his fingers behind his head and stared at his screen.

He had read Zola's email as soon as it had arrived in his inbox, and he now knew exactly what had happened. She wasn't angry that he'd been a few minutes late, she just hadn't recognised him and because of his name, she hadn't realised when he'd approached her that he'd been there for the interview.

'Still, she was unprofessional, arrogant and aggressive,' Mthunzi said, sipping sourly on his orange juice. 'And so what if you were hitting on her?' He shrugged. 'How else are you supposed to show a woman you're interested?' Mthunzi shook his head, deeply offended by this woman he had never met. 'Thank goodness she messed up the interview – I seriously doubt I could work with someone who thinks so highly of herself,' he grumbled.

Ignoring him, Mbali read through his email response again, but there was something missing. It was too cold, impersonal, but he didn't know what else he could say besides telling Zola he understood her mistake, it had happened often enough, but also that he couldn't reschedule her interview since he was about to start travelling for work.

More importantly, how could he tell her he wanted to see her *even though* he probably couldn't hire her? How could he say she had intrigued him to the extent that he'd replayed their short exchange at least twice every day in the few days since? And that common decency suggested that it would be dishonest of him to look to hire someone he couldn't stop thinking about in a *different* way.

How could he say all that and still pull back if she didn't appreciate his advances? He started:

Good morning, Zola –
Apologies for my delayed response. I am currently away travelling.
    My parents' choice in naming me has been a heavy burden, and your reaction to meeting me was in fact relatively mild.
    I suspect you will have your pick of job offers before I come back. If you haven't found one you like, I'd like to throw my hat back in the ring.
Good luck,
Mbali Thabethe

Mbali clicked the send button and hoped like crazy someone else would give Zola a job and help him avoid a complicated situation. One that would obviously be further complicated by Mthunzi's wild opinions.

But even as he sent it, he remembered the whiff of Zola's perfume as she'd got up to leave, the sweet floral scent at odds with her stormy exit. He'd noticed the roll of her hips, the flexing of her limbs against the tight material of her smart skirt.

He knew nothing about her except for her beauty and how stubborn she was. Their interaction had been practically wordless: she had seen him and left, and that was it. So why could he not just forget her?

Mthunzi was sceptical. 'I think you're just bored and making a big deal from a whole lot of nothing. You've described this girl, and it doesn't sound like there's anything special about her.'

Mbali shook his head. 'You don't get it, Mthunzi. You'd have to meet her to understand what I'm talking about, man. I can't put it into words.'

Mthunzi leant back in his chair and laughed. 'I know what *that* something special is, but you're too much of a snob to admit these types of things work. As for me, I know for a fact that witchcraft is real. She's put a spell on you, plain and simple.'

Mbali shook his head. 'You're crazy,' he chuckled. 'She doesn't even know me.'

But Mbali did know that he was a man of impressive status. People looked at him, knew just from the way he walked that his shoes were expensive; could tell instinctively that his watch cost as much as some people's entire salary. If nothing else, the car keys he put on the coffee table would have told Zola he was a man of style and obviously money.

But she hadn't been moved by the image he had so meticulously put together. Mbali was not particularly tall, but he had definite presence, announced by the musky aromatics of his cologne and punctuated by his wide shoulders and the playful jaunt of his bowed legs. His smooth milk-chocolate complexion didn't come cheap or without effort. His luscious, well-oiled beard was perfectly groomed to be thick enough to hide the shape of his jaw line, but thin enough to show off the faint indents of his dimples.

And still, Zola didn't seem moved.

He, on the other hand, had scoured Zola's social media and read her dissertation titled 'The Impact of Automation: From the Industrial Revolution to 4IR'. He'd heard something special in her voice – not in the angry tone she'd used across from him at the table, but in the calm, soothing, confident tone she'd used in a TV interview about studying abroad.

'She's actually amazing, my guy. She's smart, she's charismatic and she's not easily impressed,' Mbali said dreamily.

Mthunzi sucked his teeth and shook his head, wishing his orange juice was something stronger. 'Well, she can never work for us. What kind of boss talks about prospective employees like that?' he asked rhetorically. 'Having her anywhere near this office is an invitation for a sexual harassment suit.'

Mbali nodded thoughtfully. But he was determined to have Zola in his life one way or another. Something about Zola had taken a hold of him and just wouldn't let go.

'You're right, but you'll need to get used to the idea of having her around in other ways.'

Chapter 6

A perfect match

This time when Zola stepped out of the taxi she carefully checked for puddles first. Then the roar of thunder filled her ears and she quickly walked over to the shops that lined the opposite side of the street.

Her dress was creased and dotted with streaks of rain, but even as her umbrella buckled against the wind and flipped inside out, pouring a stream of water into her wig, Zola was determined to power through and make it in time for the interview.

Her feet slipped around in her sandals and she admitted defeat – this time; she slid them off and held them, running the rest of the way through the gate of the office park and into the tall glass building. She made it with ten minutes to spare but she was absolutely soaked – those ten minutes were crucial if she was to present herself properly.

'Hi, I'm here to see Okuhle Msimanga,' Zola announced hurriedly to the receptionist. 'Is there a bathroom nearby where I can—'

'Zola?' The rapid clicking of heels halted as a sweet voice spoke from behind her.

Zola turned slowly to find Okuhle beaming at her. She was every bit as elegant as she'd been in her photographs. Her bright-pink, wide-legged pants grazed the floor, hiding her shoes so it looked like she was floating. Okuhle's perfectly coiffed bun was like a small Afro halo behind her head, and even in the gloomy rainy weather she seemed to glow.

'Terrible weather, isn't it?' Okuhle said, taking Zola's hand. There was no awkwardness in the gesture, no coldness, no uncertainty. She nodded at the receptionist. 'Thank you, Rochelle – I'll take it from here. Come, Zola – I have a hair dryer in my office. You can get yourself together before the interview.' She guided Zola down a long corridor of glass walls.

Zola followed Okuhle down the passage coated in colourful paintings and past another reception desk towards a big office with a pink floral backdrop. It was clear Okuhle's office was an extension of her personal brand: the flowered wallpaper on the wall behind her desk, details like pot plants and books all seemed typical 'Okuhle'.

And Zola felt oddly calm around her. The woman who was going to decide whether or not Zola got a job acted and felt like an old friend.

'I'll wait for you here and we can have a do-over, okay, Zola?' Okuhle smiled, indicating the way to the loo.

Once alone, Zola replayed the awkwardness of their initial meeting. *She must think I'm an idiot*, Zola thought to herself, almost too afraid to look in the mirror and see what state she was in.

It was every bit as bad as she'd thought.

Her hair was a wet mess, the carefully curled strands a frizzy disaster. Her bare muddy feet said nothing of the look she'd so carefully created that morning. Nothing about her was impressive or professional.

Zola pulled the wig off her head and looked at it. A hair dryer couldn't fix this mess and there was no way she could redo her smudged makeup while Okuhle waited. She brushed back her neat cornrows and washed her face, but felt hopeless. This was just what she needed! She hadn't even introduced herself and already she'd messed up. Again.

Wallowing in self-pity, Zola sat down on the toilet and felt the tears roll down her cheeks. Then there was a soft knock on the door, and before she could answer, Okuhle was crouched in front of her.

'Don't cry, Zola,' she said, rubbing Zola's hand. 'Just pull yourself together and come back out. I can't hold the weather against you.' She smiled warmly before silently stepping out again.

The woman had a bit of a knack for appearing out of nowhere, Zola observed.

Zola quickly wiped her feet, slid her feet back into her sandals and, with a deep breath, walked back into Okuhle's office.

As she did, Okuhle stood up.

'Hi, I'm Okuhle Msimanga.' Okuhle offered her hand. Her smile was infectious, and Zola immediately found herself smiling back.

'Zola Khoza. Nice to meet you.'

Zola sat nervously while Okuhle looked over her CV. It was strange that she didn't remember actually applying for a job here or what she could possibly have written to motivate for a job in an events company, but here she was. And although she hadn't known anything about this place until she'd received Okuhle's email, she was now sure that this was where she wanted to work. She gulped. She hoped Okuhle didn't suddenly realise that she'd sent the interview invitation to the wrong person by accident.

'I know I don't have any events experience,' Zola said to fill the silence. 'I'm probably not qualified to do the job just yet, but I learn quickly and I know I can learn as I go,'

'Don't ever downplay your abilities, Zola,' Okuhle said sternly, but her eyes twinkled. 'You're a damn engineer. An *engineer!*'

Zola smiled nervously. This was a first – no one actually considered industrial engineers to be real engineers. Günter's mom had once told her she was an overqualified administrator.

But Okuhle seemed to be impressed.

'Firstly, the fact that you're here tells me you're tenacious and determined,' Okuhle gushed, and went on with a stream of compliments that made Zola blush. 'But seriously, our company organises elite events and conferences all over Africa. We'd be lucky to have someone with your organisational and logistical skills,' Okuhle continued, not smiling this time. 'This probably isn't the job you had in mind considering your qualifications, but we're growing, and when I saw your profile online, I knew you'd be a perfect fit. Seeing you here just sealed the deal. So, what do you say?' Okuhle raised her eyebrows.

Zola felt her eyelids flutter. People had always told her not to accept a job after the first interview, but this was perfect. Okuhle was perfect.

'I ... I don't know what to say,' Zola stammered.

Okuhle pursed her lips playfully and pulled an envelope from her desk drawer.

'Here's an offer letter – my card is in there. Call me once you've thought it over.' She stood up.

Okuhle walked Zola out to the reception area, making small talk that Zola hardly heard. Her head was buzzing and her body stiff with disbelief.

'I think that's your taxi,' Okuhle said, looking out the door at an Uber Black that was parked just outside.

The rain was pouring and Zola wished it *was* her taxi – instead, she had a long walk to the taxi rank ahead of her, a detail she didn't want to share with Okuhle. Seeing her fall apart once today was one time many.

Okuhle checked her phone. 'Ah, yes – it's the right number plate. It's definitely your taxi – just don't call it a bribe.' She winked, and hugged Zola.

In a daze, Zola climbed into the car and waved back at Okuhle. The woman was unreal, and Zola was enchanted.

By the time Zola arrived home, she still hadn't opened the envelope or even figured out how to feel about the interview. Truthfully, she was expecting to wake up any minute from a particularly delicious dream, but the envelope was still really in her hand when she climbed out of the Uber, shakily unlocked the front door and scrolled through her phone to call Günter.

The phone rang longer than usual before he answered. There was laughter in his voice.

'Hey,' Zola said, trying to sound casual.

There was music in the background and unfamiliar voices talking before she heard a door close, muffling the sound of Günter obviously having a good time. She knew it as clearly as if she were there with him: last night's drinks with friends would have turned into a party, late-night snack and more drinks, and even breakfast and before anyone could check what time it was, they were all laughing their way towards midday. He was so happy without her.

'Where are you?' Zola asked, immediately feeling like the paranoid girlfriend.

Günter sighed. 'At home. I have the day off today.' His response was short, clipped, and so unlike him.

He obviously didn't want to explain himself, wouldn't say any more about how things had changed since she'd left.

'I had an interview today,' Zola blurted out excitedly.

Günter was quiet, apparently distracted by the door opening and the giggling of a girl coming into the room. Zola couldn't make out what she was saying, but she could imagine the girl tugging on Günter, *Zola's* Günter, and whining at him to come back to the party.

'Who is that?' Zola said impatiently.

Günter sighed again, obviously irritated by the question. He chose to ignore it completely. 'How did the interview go?'

Zola felt a heaviness in her chest, her knees buckled and she just had to sit down. She felt hot, her armpits itched and her stomach swirled.

'So much better than I expected,' she said trying to sound unbothered, but her voice cracked.

'Tell her to call back,' the girl whispered loudly enough now for Zola to hear.

A lump formed in Zola's throat. Her dress suddenly felt tight and uncomfortable. Something was going on.

'Can I call you back?' Günter said after a pause in which it sounded like he was … giggling?

Was she tickling him? Was Günter letting this girl *tickle* him? Zola tried to place the voice. She didn't think it was someone she knew, but there was something familiar …

The accent. She was South African.

Zola could hear her breath quicken.

'Zola?' Günter said impatiently. 'Listen, I'll call you back,' he said laughing again.

'Don't bother.' Zola hung up.

Chapter 7

Guess it's over

When Thobile came into the kitchen, Zola was sitting at the table, her eyes dry, red and scratchy. The sealed envelope sat untouched in front of her.

Thobile decided to follow her mother's advice and be gentle with her sister. 'Another bad interview?'

Zola sighed heavily and pushed the envelope across the table.

'No.' The heady feeling she'd had as she left the Larger Than Life offices with Okuhle smiling warmly from behind the glass door was so far gone that she couldn't even conjure it enough to tell Thobile about it. So she stuck to the facts: 'The interview was great. The offices were beautiful. Okuhle is wonderful and she offered me the job on the spot,' Zola said without any joy, her voice dry and monotonous.

Confused, Thobile took it upon herself to carefully open the envelope.

'Zola? Zola, have you read this?' Thobile asked a few moments later, scouring the contract for an error.

'No.' Zola sighed. 'I haven't read the contract, but I'll take the job. It's not like I have anything better to do.'

Thobile shook her head and stood up to switch on the overhead light before checking the contract again.

'Okay, okay, okay. There's a non-disclosure agreement here so obviously you'll be dealing with some juicy details on the job, and they're offering you thirty-five thousand rand as a starting salary, with medical aid, pension – oh my gosh, Zola!' Thobile squealed and jumped up to hug her sister. 'This is just in time for my matric dance!'

For her sister's sake, Zola mustered a small smile and pretended to be interested in Thobile's lofty ideas: the Swarovski crystals she wanted scattered like stars over the hem of her full-length dress and the sneakers she'd have designed and made specifically for the night. It was nice to see Thobile so happy, not because she'd ever been unhappy, but because Zola herself hadn't been happy at her age. She had worried and studied, hadn't made any meaningful friendships and hadn't even attended her own matric dance. She'd thought it was a stupid waste of time and money, but seeing Thobile so excited, she now wished she had gone.

'So, what were you crying about?' Thobile asked, finally sitting down with an onion and a chopping board. 'Your life is great! I wish I had everything as put together as you do.'

Zola raised an eyebrow and managed a chuckle. 'Put together?'

Her life seemed anything but put together. Her plans had changed and then failed, and just as one thing got better, another got worse. Now she had a job offer but Günter, the person she'd always shared everything with, didn't want to hear about it.

'I think Günter is seeing someone else,' Zola confessed in disbelief. Even hearing herself say it was shocking.

'But, Zola, you have a life here too,' Thobile said. 'I mean, *of course* you guys are going to grow apart. You'll have your friends and he'll have his friends ... There's no way you'll know everything that's happening in his life from all the way over here.'

But Zola didn't *want* a life here – this was all just temporary, or it was supposed to be. She was just trying to find a way to make it work. She was still completely committed to finding her way back to Germany and Günter.

'The long-distance thing never works,' Thobile said with all the wisdom of her seventeen years as she set about starting to cook their supper.

Zola felt a stab in her chest. Thobile's random commentary on relationships was irritating. What did Thobile know about anything? She was basically a child; she knew nothing about relationships. High school wasn't the real world, and whatever she thought she knew was obviously wrong.

A sharp searing pain shot up to her throat and sent hot tears running down her cheeks. 'Says who?' she spat. 'How would *you* know?'

'*Everyone* knows,' Thobile said, cubing potatoes with practised speed and tossing them into a hot frying pan.

Zola tilted her head and watched Thobile, who suddenly seemed older. *Even a broken clock was right twice a day*, thought Zola. Maybe Thobile was right about the long-distance thing. It sounded like something that was true.

'Well, I didn't,' Zola whispered and left to go stand outside – the smell of tinned pilchards had filled the small kitchen and wafted through the house.

Zola understood the big things, the things she thought were important, but she didn't always get people. Why didn't they just do what they said they would do? Günter had said he would be miserable without her. That he'd be counting the hours until they could be together again. And yet it seemed he was not only happy, but he was also losing track of time.

The rest of the evening went by with Zola in a daze. The food her mother insisted Thobile add too much salt and too many spices to was tasteless. Nomsebenzi's praises of Thobile's cooking were a swirl of high-pitched talking and clapping until after dinner, when Zola was left alone and numb sitting on her bed.

She looked through the many pictures she had of her and Günter on her phone. She read through the text messages they'd exchanged when she'd first come home, both sure she would be back in Germany and in his arms in a matter of weeks.

She couldn't help but laugh bitterly as her fingers began to move frantically over her keypad: a long text to Günter telling him exactly how she felt, of her disappointment and her anguish.

And, of course, just how done they were.

Okuhle slid her car into a parking spot at the airport. The floral notes of her perfume blew back at her and she wondered for a second if she'd overdone it. She wanted this to be perfect.

Her life was coming together. Her business was growing, she was surrounding herself with hopeful and talented people, and the love of her life was coming home.

Okuhle checked her face in the rear-view mirror and then looked down at her outfit. Casual, unassuming – the kind of outfit you wear when you aren't trying to prove anything. She'd spent hours putting it together.

She took a breath, hopped out of her car and strutted through the airport doors, hiding how anxious and unsure she felt of absolutely everything at this point.

She knew he wouldn't be expecting her. It wouldn't occur to him that she'd be the one to collect him from the airport, but there she'd be. She had always been there one way or another, but surely now he would see her for what she was: not his childhood friend, not an old flame and definitely not a sister.

None of those roles matched the throbbing in her heart as she spotted him striding through the sliding doors at Arrivals. She walked towards him.

He didn't see her at first, and then there was a flicker of recognition, a small smile spreading across his face. His skin glowed, his head gleamed smooth. He seemed happy to see her.

Okuhle's heart was pounding in her chest; every beat all but shook her body. She didn't hear the chaos of announcements and greetings and phone calls happening around her – all she could hear was the rush of blood in her head, the hum of fear taking control.

This was not the first time Okuhle had expected things to go well, not the first time she'd expected her happily ever after and ended up with a broken heart.

Everyone had expected their teenage love affair to end at the altar.

Their relationship had played out like a slideshow: pictures from their shared baptism followed by childhood birthday parties and family gatherings, right up to their matric dance and the first overseas trips they took with each other's families. It was as if their families had been preparing for this union all their lives, and obviously Okuhle had thought about the wedding for as long as she could remember, collecting ideas on Pinterest, and adding new trends over the years.

Then, out of the blue, and before she'd even realised it, it had all ended.

There'd been no back and forth, no big fight, no long talks. It was as if while she wasn't looking they had just drifted apart, and she hadn't noticed until he was so far gone there was nothing left to put back together. They were both so ambitious and they'd been so busy – excelling at their studies and then building businesses ... So focused on building their perfect life together that they seemed to have simply stopped talking to each other.

For him, friendship was the only logical way forward.

'You're like a sister to me, Okuhle. I'd hate to lose you just because our parents' ridiculous fantasy didn't come true,' he'd said from across the dinner table.

Okuhle's breath had caught in her throat and she'd almost choked. At that point she'd been expecting a cheesy proposal, not a casual break-up. Their parents' 'ridiculous fantasy' was hers too – and no, she didn't want to be anything like a sister to him.

Okuhle had smiled through her heartbreak. She'd stayed calm and listened to her mother's advice – and his mother's advice too. She hadn't freaked out or got angry. Her strategy would be to stay close – maybe even indispensable – until he got over this little phase he was going through.

And now here she was, waiting to greet him at the airport.

Okuhle felt her cheeks tighten into a smile. She had stayed the course and now she hoped against hope that his smile would hold the sweetness of young love again, the promise of romance. As he dropped his bags and held her close, the woody smell of his cologne filled her nostrils and made her weak.

'Hi, Okuhle. Thanks for picking me up.'

She melted into his arms and almost forgot everything.

'Hi, Mbali. How was your trip?'

Chapter 8

Two single ladies

As soon as Mbali hugged her, Okuhle knew that nothing had changed. He was still all boyish charm and overly comfortable familiarity – but even as she slipped into his arms, she recognised that something seemed to be holding him back.

The only one visibly uncomfortable with the whole situation was his sidekick, Mthunzi, who never seemed to leave Mbali for a second.

'So I'm the third wheel now?' he asked, coming up behind them with the luggage trolley and hanging a heavy arm over Okuhle's shoulder. 'You couldn't bring a friend for me to cuddle?'

Knowing Mbali didn't feel the way she did, her body stayed stiff against his. Even with his arm pulling her close enough she could feel his hips move with each step, it was clear to Okuhle that his mind didn't drift towards passion as hers did. What might look from the outside like intimacy felt like nothing more than the habit of a deep and long-formed friendship – the same familiarity that had led him to introduce

Okuhle over and over again as the sister he'd never had.

Had he *always* loved her as he would a sister? Had their passion been nothing more than the excitement of youth? He'd never actually asked if she'd felt the same way about him as he had about her – he'd just assumed he was speaking for both of them when he'd said they were better as friends.

'You know, Okuhle, you should have come to Dubai with us. Your types were all over the place,' Mbali announced later, as they finished their dinner at a restaurant near the airport. Mbali offered Okuhle his plate to pick at – as usual she had ordered a dry salad, but now wanted his steak and chips.

How rude, Okuhle thought to herself even as she smiled at him. For years she had hidden her hurt and pretended to be okay with his carelessness.

'I didn't know I had a type,' she laughed.

Mthunzi guzzled his beer and motioned over a waitress for another refill.

'You know the ones? Sophisticated types, fitted designer suits, subtle accessories that probably cost as much as a small house and custom-blended cologne.' Mbali laughed loudly, throwing back his head and showing off his Adam's apple and bright-white teeth. 'How well do I know you, hey?' he asked, gently nudging Okuhle.

Okuhle was increasingly convinced that he was laughing at her, not with her.

'Too well,' she said softly, her bright smile finally retiring as she sipped her sparkling water, letting the bubbles fizz on her tongue.

Mbali had just described himself. *He* was her type, and he knew it. And yet here he was, overplaying the big-brother bit.

'You really should have come with us, Hlehle, even if it was just for the break. You need it. You work too hard,' he said gently.

Mthunzi rolled his eyes. 'If anyone needs a break, it's me. *I* work too hard keeping my food down listening to the two of you,' he said bitterly.

The rest of the hour was spent in the same old way: Mbali and Mthunzi regaling each other with stories of Mbali's glory days on the rugby field. When Mbali got to the bit where he could have been Siya Kolisi before Siya Kolisi, it was the last straw for Okuhle.

She yawned and stretched out languidly. 'I'm going to need to get to bed if I'm going to make it in time for yoga in the morning.'

As usual Mbali insisted on driving them home in Okuhle's car. Then Okuhle insisted she could drop off Mbali (and Mthunzi) and drive herself the short distance from his apartment to her townhouse and call him when she got home. He let her win, of course – it avoided the awkwardness of him being at her house.

Okuhle could clearly see how Mbali felt about her.

She *had* tried to forget him. But her obsession with Mbali was like a drug, and her mother was her most reliable dealer. If her mother said they would end up together, it had to be true, right?

Okuhle couldn't help but love Mbali, and she would warp her world until she could see a version of reality in which he loved her too.

'Bra, you need to stop including me in this weirdness with Okuhle,' Mthunzi complained before her custom-painted bright-yellow Mustang had even turned the corner.

Mbali sighed deeply and led the way to the lift.

'Dude, you can speak to my mom about that. I don't know why she keeps sending Okuhle mixed messages and orchestrating these dinners – as if the more I see her, the more I will miraculously realise that I've always loved her.'

Mbali knew about his mother's plan. She'd been overjoyed when he and Okuhle had started dating and had bent all the rules to help their relationship along. And even though his father was normally disinterested and uninvolved in such things, his interest had been piqued when Okuhle and Mbali had continued to date through university.

If it had been any other girl, his parents would have behaved very differently. Maybe that's why he'd let it go on as long as it did. He'd played the perfect boyfriend long after they'd been deemed 'such a cute couple' by all their teenage friends. And there were expectations: Okuhle had openly discussed their wedding, and his mother referred to Okuhle as her daughter. A clean break had been impossible – there was no way he could just be done with it. Okuhle and both their mothers' hopes for a happily ever after would always hang over his head.

And it wasn't like he didn't care; she really was like a sister to him.

He knew she didn't share that feeling. It was clear she was still holding onto hope. But he said it over and over again, maybe to convince her that it was true – or better yet, to give up the youthful dream they had both diligently been fed over the years.

It was clear to Mbali: he and Okuhle were not meant to be.

On her first day at work, Zola arrived to an empty office.

She'd hardly been able to sleep the previous night. Excited and anxious all at once, she had sat up in bed every hour or so to check the time until she could reasonably get up.

Now in the still, cool room, she could take it all in. Zola spun around laughing softly to herself. This truly felt like a scene from a movie.

'You're early.' Okuhle walked up briskly behind her. 'I usually have the office to myself in the morning.'

Okuhle's smile didn't quite reach her eyes. She was not like how Zola remembered her from three weeks ago; there was no glow or ethereal sense of peace and balance. Today Okuhle looked like a tired office worker who would rather be somewhere else.

'I'll show you the coffee station. You're going to need it,' Okuhle said, indicating ahead.

Okuhle was wearing strappy sandals and a plain yellow dress. She was shorter without her heels, and the bouncing Afro that had looked like a halo when they'd first met was rolled up in wool and braided back in two lines. With her dewy face, Okuhle looked sweet and childlike, and even though she seemed sad, Zola found herself smiling back whenever Okuhle looked at her.

'I really love your enthusiasm, Zola, but I'm afraid your first day is going to be crazy. I received a call yesterday and I couldn't refuse the job – we need to put together a one-day African Wedding Expo in just three weeks.' Okuhle sighed. 'Please, have a seat so I can brief you.'

Zola sat down on an armchair next to a small table where Okuhle was setting out their coffees. She took a sip. The coffee was black with no sugar. She liked hers sweet with milk, but didn't have it in her just then to tell Okuhle, even though Okuhle was adding one heaped teaspoon after the next to her own coffee.

'I wish I had something more interesting for you to sink your teeth into first, but we roll with the punches.' Okuhle smiled, stirring her sweet coffee.

'You don't like weddings?' Zola asked. 'I mean, the African Wedding Expo is the first of its kind. Showing off the traditional elements of African weddings across the continent – that's pretty exciting.'

'Well, someone's done their homework.' Okuhle looked up at Zola over her cup.

Zola blushed. She had read up on every expo expected this year and tried to imagine which ones Larger Than Life would be involved in. The African Wedding Expo had been one of the most highly anticipated.

'Call me jaded. The idea of putting together the perfect African wedding makes me feel a bit sick right now,' Okuhle said, twisting her face. 'But a little jealousy isn't a bad thing, right?'

Zola was so surprised that for a moment she forgot herself. 'I honestly can't imagine anything you could be jealous of, Okuhle.' The woman clearly had it all. And if she really wanted to get married, she could no doubt do it tomorrow.

'Not so. I am a reluctantly single woman neck-deep in all things wedding. I'm sorry, I …' Okuhle's eyes became watery. 'I shouldn't have said that. Consider this a sensitive subject.'

'You and me both,' said Zola, hoping to close the subject but still be comforting. Okuhle flashed a smile of appreciation.

As if on cue, the office started to fill up with new faces. Amongst the incoming bevy of colleagues came the receptionist Zola had seen on the day of her interview, her arms burdened with an over-the-top bouquet of flowers.

'Hi, Zola – I'm Rochelle. These flowers are for you,' she said excitedly. 'Someone must be missing you already!'

Zola took the flowers, certain there had been a mistake.

Okuhle clapped her hands in disbelief. 'And just as you were telling me how single you are!'

'Err …' Confused, Zola read the card. 'They're from an … acquaintance. Please, you have them, Okuhle,' she offered, handing them over. 'I hope they make your day a little happier. And as for me, I'm keen to settle in!'

Zola stood up and headed for what was clearly her desk. It was hard to miss: it was the one with the huge 'Welcome' balloon floating above it and a gift basket waiting for her. In the basket she found a collection of gorgeous stationery and various tubes of hand creams and lip glosses. *So thoughtful*, she thought to herself. Almost as a last-minute addition, a laptop bag with its price tag still attached leant against the side of her cubicle.

As she looked up, Zola realised that she had a clear view of Okuhle's office, and Okuhle had a clear view of her.

After finishing her coffee, Okuhle walked across the office with the huge bouquet, a mix of all her favourites. She loved flowers – everyone knew that – and even though these hadn't been meant for her, they would definitely brighten her day.

Once at her desk, she put the flowers in a vase and arranged them nicely, pulling out the card to throw it away – though she couldn't resist reading the mysterious message that had left her new employee so baffled.

Zola,
I knew you'd have yourself sorted before I even came back.
   Good luck on your first day!
– Mbali Thabethe

Okuhle froze.
   Why would Mbali be sending flowers to *Zola*?

Chapter 9

Small world

Okuhle felt her legs shake. Her knees had turned to jelly and her head felt too heavy for her neck. How could this be happening?

She stared at the card in her hands. It was definitely Mbali's handwriting, with the loops all sloping to the left. Surely there had been a mistake? These were *her* favourite flowers. But the card was definitely addressed to Zola.

The whole thing made her sick.

Okuhle picked up her phone and dialled Mbali's number. While it rang, she wondered what she could say.

This wasn't an accident – he knew exactly what he was doing. Her office wasn't big, she'd just hired Zola herself and she would obviously notice a bouquet of her favourite flowers on Zola's desk. And did they *have* to be her favourites? He clearly hadn't considered her feelings.

Okuhle knew that Mbali could be self-centred, but this was beyond hurtful. It was like he had taken aim and opened fire.

And there was Zola right now, sitting at her desk in *Okuhle*'s offices, surrounded by *Okuhle*'s IT people helping her to get settled. And getting flowers from *Okuhle*'s man! A man who clearly no longer wanted her. A man who thought so little of her that he was sending his new love interest *Okuhle*'s favourite flowers, knowing that she would see them!

No answer from Mbali. She cut the call and scrolled down past Mbali's mother's number and Mthunzi's number to her best friend, Terry's, number. It rang only once before Terry answered. It really sucked that Terry now lived in Cape Town.

'Terry, I honestly hate him,' Okuhle said, putting her head down on her desk. 'You will not believe what he's done now …'

The thing was, counting all of Mbali's wrongs didn't make Okuhle want him any less. It never had. She and Terry slipped into their regular routine of listing Mbali's failings and had got as far back as the time Mbali and Mthunzi had thought it would be funny to throw her into a swimming pool fully clothed on her fifteenth birthday, when Zola knocked on her door.

'She's here,' Okuhle hissed. 'I'll call you back.'

She took three deep breaths that did nothing to prepare her before asking Zola to come in.

'Are you okay?' Zola asked. 'Your eyes are red.'

'Don't worry about it. We've got tons of work to get through,' Okuhle said coldly, and deftly opened a number of files on her laptop. 'Keep in mind that all these files are confidential and property of Larger Than Life as stated in your signed NDA,' Okuhle said without looking at Zola. 'I would have liked to have given you a soft introduction to the industry seeing as you have no experience at all, but changes of plan are the nature of this beast called event management.'

Her nails clicked on the keyboard as she sent one file after the other to Zola's newly set-up company email.

'Khanyisa, our office manager, will brief you on what needs to be done today. And, Zola? This company is my baby. Don't let me down.'

Okuhle dismissed Zola with a wave of her hand.

She hadn't even let Zola speak. Zola felt herself shrink as she walked back over to her desk to read the files. Everything seemed straightforward, but she was nervous so she went to find Khanyisa for the guidance Okuhle was so certain she needed.

After asking around a bit, she found Khanyisa's desk, right back next to hers.

'What's wrong, new girl?' Khanyisa smiled knowingly. 'You met the real Okuhle?'

Zola shrugged and remembered how her mother had warned her never to speak ill of her boss, especially with her colleagues. That was not the kind of drama she needed in her life and besides, Okuhle hadn't actually been nasty to her – she was just being the boss. It was something Zola would need to get used to.

'Nothing's wrong,' Zola said, forcing a smile. 'I'm just a little overwhelmed.'

Khanyisa nodded kindly and went over the tasks for the day. The first thing they needed to do was secure a venue for the event, compare quotes and go through the logistics of transport, catering and the requirements of the exhibitors.

'You know she only got the gig because her mother, the Minister of Miscommunication herself, is friends with the Minister of Tourism, right?' Khanyisa whispered bitterly. 'That's why she does the whole sisterhood-thing and gets super-friendly from time to time. She's easing her guilt.' Khanyisa pursed her lips.

'I didn't know that,' Zola said carefully. She didn't want to add to this conversation. And that was of course how most things worked. Even with her limited experience of the job market, she knew it wasn't *what* you knew but *who* you knew.

'Well, Zola, now you know. Okuhle's not your friend – she's your boss. She's just tolerating you for the numbers. And sooner or later she'll have you giving press snippets about how she pulled you from the dark abyss of poverty by giving you a chance to be mentored by her.' Khanyisa raised her eyebrows.

During her research on her would-be boss, Zola had read the articles where an intern, maybe Khanyisa herself, had said something similar about Okuhle. And Zola had been floored by her future boss's graciousness. One thing was for sure though: Okuhle definitely wasn't her friend, and Zola would be sure to remember it.

Zola worked diligently through her lunch break and before she knew it, it was five o'clock and the office was almost empty. She looked up and saw her last three colleagues leave. And then it was just her and Okuhle.

Glancing through the glass wall that separated Okuhle from her staff, Zola caught Okuhle watching her, a thoughtful expression on her face at first, and then a smile.

Zola felt unsettled, unsure if she should pack up and leave or if she should stay at her desk and work long enough for Okuhle to see how dedicated she was.

'Let's not have people thinking I'm exploiting you,' Okuhle said, as if reading her mind. She walked towards Zola. 'You did well today, sis. Let's call it a day.'

Zola smiled, not knowing how to take the compliment with her newfound understanding about her boss. She began packing up her desk with Okuhle standing over her, watching her every move, as if to make sure Zola wasn't taking anything she shouldn't. It was awkward.

'How do you know Mbali Thabethe?' Okuhle finally asked.

Zola had already forgotten the flowers with the card that was probably still tucked into the bouquet. It was strange that he'd sent them to her, and she wasn't sure how she felt about it. But what with setting up her new workspace, signing the HR paperwork, getting set up by IT and getting to grips with the project, she hadn't exactly had much time to think about it.

'I don't really *know* him know him,' Zola explained. 'I almost met him for an interview, but things went wrong. I basically walked out on him. It's so embarrassing.'

Smiling, Okuhle pulled up a chair and rested her elbows on the desk next to Zola.

'Tell me about it.'

'Well ...' Zola laughed remembering that awful incident at the coffee shop. 'We were supposed to meet at Milk and Cookies in Rosebank for the interview, and I sat waiting and waiting because I was early, not because he was late.'

Okuhle nodded. 'And I bet you had to ward off all those would-be sugar daddies that always hang out there.'

'Exactly!' Zola gasped covering her face. 'And you see, I thought I was waiting for a woman named Mbali, so when a man pulled up and sat across from me, I thought it was one of those guys and I got angry and I left before he could introduce himself.'

Okuhle laughed and slapped Zola's hand. 'Oh my gosh! And then what? Did he chase after you and explain who he was?'

'No,' Zola squealed. 'He just sat there, and I left, fully left, and I was *livid*. I thought my interviewer hadn't bothered to come and meet me.'

'Oh geez.' Okuhle shook her head still laughing as she came round to the real question: 'But why is he sending you flowers?'

Zola shrugged. 'I don't know. Maybe he's feeling guilty because as soon as I got home and I realised I'd made a mistake, I emailed him to apologise and asked to reschedule, but he wasn't available. And then you emailed me and here I am.'

Zola had left out the part where she'd agonised for days over him not replying to her email – but that was history. All she'd wanted was a job, and now she had one. In her opinion, the Mbali Thabethe chapter of her life had been short, and was now over.

'I don't blame you, though,' Okuhle said. 'Mbali is a really odd name for a boy. He got teased about it all through high school.'

'Oh. You went to the same high school?' Zola asked, glancing at the darkening sky beyond the window. Her bag was already packed but she didn't want to leave Okuhle hanging.

'Yeah,' Okuhle said, her casual tone now slightly forced. Zola could tell she hadn't meant to reveal that she had a history with Mbali. 'Same preschool, primary school and high school. Our parents move in the same circles.'

They sat in an awkward silence for a moment more until Zola picked up her bag.

Okuhle touched her arm gently.

'He shouldn't be sending you flowers. I mean, he doesn't know you, right? You aren't even friends?'

For some reason, Zola felt nervous. What was Okuhle saying? Was Mbali married? Why else would someone like him have no business sending women flowers at work?

'Oh,' Zola said lightly. 'Like I said, he probably just felt bad for not giving me a second chance.'

Okuhle sighed and shook her head. 'Men like Mbali don't feel bad about anything, and they definitely don't send flowers for no reason.' She looked meaningfully at Zola.

Zola didn't have much else to say, but it seemed that Okuhle wasn't finished.

'Have you spoken to him today since he sent you the flowers?' Okuhle pursed her lips.

An uneasiness settled over Zola. Clearly she had done something wrong, and she wanted a way to fix it. To stay in Okuhle's good graces. She wasn't sure what kind of man Mbali was, but it was clear he wasn't the kind of man she should be casually associated with.

'No, I thought I'd just send him an email to thank him when I got home,' Zola said nervously.

Okuhle smiled. 'Let me help you with that. Give me your phone.'

Reluctantly, Zola pulled her phone out of her bag, unlocked it, set it to 'compose email' and handed it to Okuhle.

Okuhle was all smiles as she typed, nodded to herself as she silently reread what she'd written and added a little more.

'And … send,' she said proudly. And then almost as an afterthought: 'You've made it clear that you aren't interested in his advances or his friendship.'

Zola was confused. She hadn't even been aware of Mbali's advances or his attempts at friendship. And why would he want to be friends with her anyway? Too dazed to even question what Okuhle had put in the email, she took back her phone and returned it to her bag.

'Um … It's really late. I should get going before the taxis to Vosloo finish.'

'I forgot about that. I'll walk you out.' Okuhle smiled as she guided Zola to the exit.

What the hell was that all about? Zola wondered as she walked out of the building and into Sandton's dark streets. Okuhle had seemed happy enough after the email had been sent – and that was a good thing, right?

Zola dared not pull out her phone while she was walking. She'd have to wait to find out exactly what Okuhle had said to Mbali on her behalf.

Chapter 10

Unkind regards

Mbali read Zola's email and almost choked on his whisky. Sitting in a dimly lit cigar lounge waiting for his friends, he'd imagined that round about now he would be excusing himself to go and see her. It was a simple formula: he would send the flowers, she'd gush her thanks, they'd set up a date and he'd win her over.

There had been some variation, but it had always worked. Until now.

Because Zola's email had basically said that their interaction wasn't personal enough to be offensive, and not effective enough to be impressive. She was simply not interested.

'No way,' he muttered searching through their email thread for her phone number. He found it, and dialled without a second thought.

'Hello?' Zola's voice sounded unsure, almost a whisper.

'I'm not sure how to address you after your email,' Mbali greeted her.

'Sorry, who is this?'

Having never spoken to her on the phone, Mbali knew he should have introduced himself. Instead, stung, he started reading Zola's email: '*Good evening, Mr Thabethe. I would like to extend my gratitude for your support and congratulations during my job search ...*'

'The email.'

Clearly she now knew who he was.

Mbali laughed. 'You know you can tell me to fuck off without all this professional courtesy. The flowers themselves weren't a professional gesture. I'm trying to get to *know* you.'

Zola's only reply was to sigh heavily into the phone.

'I won't lie, that email caught me off guard. Sending the flowers was a gamble, but I do hope you liked them.'

Zola sighed again. 'Sorry about the email,' she said. 'The flowers were beautiful and ... unexpected.'

Mbali wasn't used to being on the back foot. Clearly Zola wasn't as easy to impress as he was used to. She clearly wasn't excited by the flowers – he'd searched her social media pages today and she hadn't even posted pictures of them.

And she was cold, no giddiness over his call. Not even a little excitement. Zola was different, not the kind of girl he usually went for. The type who knew who he was without introduction, knew what his watch was worth and unapologetically wanted some of that.

Zola intrigued him.

'So? How was your first day?' Mbali asked cautiously. The possibility of being rejected at any moment was thrilling even.

'It was great, thanks. Hit the ground running, but I'm really grateful for the opportunity.'

She was being careful, guarded. Even though Mbali didn't know Zola very well, their earlier emails had felt friendlier.

Or maybe he had made more of them than there actually was?

'Well, I'm glad,' Mbali said awkwardly. With so little to work with, what else could he say?

Zola sighed again. He was obviously boring her or irritating her –

either way, she didn't appear to want to be on the phone with him.

'Thank you.' On her end of the phone, Zola struggled with how to end the call. 'Um … Sorry, I'm actually in a taxi home right now. I have to go. But … I appreciate you calling. Bye.' She hung up without even waiting for him to reply.

'Bra, that was sickening.' Mthunzi approached with two drinks in his hands.

Mbali cringed. 'You heard that?'

'We all did.' Their friend Thapelo sat down. 'So we moved away as far as possible until you were done.' He shivered. 'I don't even want to know if what you've got is contagious.'

Mbali nodded. His attempt to try and start something with Zola was pathetic. And it had failed. Which only seemed to make him want her more.

'You guys don't get it – the thrill of the chase.' Mbali laughed to console himself. Zola didn't even seem to know he was chasing her. That alone made Mbali wonder about her, and the more he thought about her, the more every little detail he knew about her thrilled him. She was what he wanted to be. Everything she had, although he knew it couldn't be very much, she'd gotten on her own. He didn't really know anyone like that. As unreasonable as it was, he wanted more than anything to understand her.

'Let me put you guys in the picture since Mbali here is obviously too ashamed to.' Mthunzi started: 'Mbali was supposed to recruit Miss Attitude to do our logistics, but she messed up the interview so Mbali couldn't offer her the job.' Mthunzi shrugged. 'But she's hot, so now he's chasing her and acting like an idiot.'

'What the hell, bra?' Thapelo laughed. 'If she's not interested, there are many girls who are. Cut your losses, man.'

Mbali glared at Mthunzi. 'Don't you guys get tired of being with women who don't like you?' he countered. 'Seriously, do you think these women who don't bother getting to know you actually *like* you?'

Thapelo and Mthunzi both flung up their hands. And Mbali had to be honest: as long as he'd got what he wanted, being liked had never mattered to him either.

But now that he'd met Zola … Well, he really wanted her to like him. And that made no sense, not even to him.

Mbali scanned through his Instagram feed. Maybe she had posted the flowers now. Maybe she just hadn't wanted to be on social media while at work. Maybe …

'Bloody hell!' He slammed his phone onto the table, picked up his drink and drained it. Mthunzi and Thapelo stared at him.

'Tell me why *Okuhle* has the flowers I sent to *Zola*?' Mbali exploded. 'Tell me that?'

Mthunzi picked up Mbali's phone and quickly scanned Okuhle's caption about sisterhood and loyalty. He chuckled to himself.

'Because Zola *gave* them to Okuhle,' he explained patiently. 'I'm telling you, bra, that girl Okuhle has tricks. She probably saw the flowers and found a way to make Zola hand them over.'

Thapelo stared at Mbali accusingly. 'So this girl knows *Okuhle*?'

For the second time that evening Mbali was embarrassed.

'I saw an update on Zola's LinkedIn page. She *works* for Okuhle. It's not like they're actually friends,' he explained.

'That's even worse, man.' Thapelo took a long drink of his beer. 'Why don't you just go back to Okuhle? She's smart, beautiful and it's obvious she's still crazy about you.' He picked up his jacket and made to leave. 'Anyway, I'll leave you bachelors to it. I have a hot meal and an even hotter wife waiting at home for me.'

Mbali shook his head. Thapelo had done what every parent wanted: he'd married the girl they liked and he seemed happy enough. Maybe Mbali could have gone back to Okuhle, maybe he still would if she'd just leave him alone for a moment.

Okuhle was too available. Mbali knew he could call her right now and she'd rush right over. She was hoarding-a-bouquet-that-wasn't-even-meant-for-her level of desperate. It was too much.

'You know, I'm not exactly a member of Okuhle's fan club but, bra, the flowers? Mxm. That was cold,' Mthunzi said, kissing his teeth. 'Why would you send flowers to Okuhle's office for another woman? I bet she lost her shit.'

Maybe she had lost it. Maybe she'd screamed at Zola and taken the flowers from her. That would have been a real scene ... Okuhle could get a bit crazy. And if Mbali had any chance with Zola, he would need to fix this.

The evening dragged on with Mthunzi drinking more than he should, his argument for Mbali to just fix things with Okuhle becoming weaker with every drink: 'She gets you, Mbali. She's always understood you, even when you didn't understand yourself ...' Soon it became: 'Lishen, bra, even your mom loveesh her and your mom hatesh everyone.'

It was time to call it a night.

'Let's go. I'll drop you off,' said Mbali, dragging Mthunzi out to the car park.

'You know what your problem ish, Mbali ...?' Mthunzi started up again, a predictable beginning for a senseless argument. 'Your problem ish ... you don't take me sherioushly. You don't shee me ...' he slurred, ducking into the car but banging his head in the process. 'I'm your friend and I'm trying to give advice, but you don't even lishen to me ...' Mthunzi fumbled with his seatbelt. 'Forget Mish Attitude ... It'sh not like Okuhle ish going anywhere ...'

Chapter 11

Can't keep a good man down

On her second day, Zola arrived for work before anyone else and settled straight away at her desk. She had a long list of things she wanted to check off her to-do list before she went home. And she fully intended to leave on time after the terror of walking the streets of downtown Jozi alone the evening before.

It wasn't too long before her colleagues started arriving.

'Hey, sis,' Khanyisa grinned, and leant down too close to rest her elbows on Zola's chair.

'Hi!' It was an awkward position, but Zola made a conscious effort to be friendly. She'd been told more than once that she was cold, distant.

'What are you busy with?' Khanyisa asked.

Zola's first instinct was to ask what business it was of Khanyisa's. Instead, she smiled and listed some of the many things she needed to do in the hopes that she'd be left to do her work in peace. 'It's a lot, and I'm working on a really tight timeline. I'm sorry if I seem aloof,' Zola said.

Still smiling, Khanyisa looked over Zola's shoulder and read from her screen.

'You know your boss isn't coming in today, right?' Khanyisa asked. 'She's working from home so she can be in "homeostasis",' Khanyisa mimicked Okuhle's accent.

'Oh.' Zola felt a sense of relief. Even though she still liked Okuhle, the business with the email and then Mbali's phone call had left her tense – so tense that Zola had only read 'her' email once she was comfortably in bed at home and everyone else was asleep.

Okuhle's email was definitely not what Zola had had in mind as a response to Mbali's unexpected gesture. It had bordered on rude, but there was nothing that could be done about that now.

For the next couple of hours Zola zoned in on her work and blitzed through her list of tasks, and before she knew it, it was lunch time. She took her lunch box from her bag and made her way to the microwave.

She was waiting for her food to heat up when Rochelle from reception hurriedly came in.

'Has anyone seen Zola?'

Zola turned, only to find the eyes of the entire office staff on her – as Mbali stepped towards her with an even bigger bouquet of flowers in his arms.

The room was silent. Zola could hear her heart throbbing in her ears.

Mbali sidestepped Rochelle and strode towards her, the smell of his cologne reaching Zola before he did.

He smiled. 'I noticed your flowers had made their way to someone else's desk yesterday, so I thought I'd replace them.'

Zola took the bouquet with shaking hands. What the hell was going on here? Why was Mbali here with more flowers, and how did he know she'd given the first bouquet to Okuhle?

'Thank you,' she stammered.

Zola looked around for a place to put the flowers until Khanyisa took them and found a vase for her, winking at Zola suggestively.

THE THING WITH ZOLA

Awkwardly, Zola and Mbali watched as Khanyisa arranged the flowers and placed them on Zola's desk.

'You really didn't have to come all this way—' Zola started.

'Oh, but I did,' Mbali cut her off, his hand on her arm making the space between them smaller. 'How else was I going to see you again?'

'Thank you. Um ... let me walk you out.'

'So, how are you finding it here?' Mbali asked as they weaved through the strangely quiet office.

Zola wanted to hide under a rock – it was clear everyone was listening to every word she said. 'It's okay,' she said in little more than a whisper. 'I'm still getting used to everything, but everyone seems nice.'

Walking half a step behind Mbali, she was able to take him in. Everything about him was perfectly presented and in place – from his shiny shoes to the very top of his head, where there was not a single hair. The gold watch gleaming from his wrist matched his small, understated belt buckle and the cufflinks on his designer shirt.

What kind of man wears cufflinks in the middle of the week? Zola thought, aware that she was trotting to keep up with his long strides.

'They do seem nice, and you seem busy,' Mbali said, eventually pausing to walk side by side with Zola. 'I also brought you lunch. I kind of guessed I wouldn't be able to lure you too far from your desk.'

When he smiled, his teeth were perfectly white and gleaming, his incisors slightly pointed.

Attractive, thought Zola, despite herself, and found herself blushing.

'I was just about to eat actually,' Zola said, thinking about the Tupperware of pap and wors she'd left in the microwave.

'Great, then eat with me,' Mbali said unlocking his sports car with the touch of a button. Zola tried to figure out what kind of car it was – she knew her sister would want all the details. Mbali pulled a shopping bag out of the boot, pressed a button to close it again and headed over to a picnic table and bench that was set up on the shady side of the car park. Zola had never noticed it before, but Mbali clearly knew his way around.

He set down the bag and pulled out two chicken salads and two bottles of ginger beer, and laid them on the table.

'I didn't know what you liked so I guessed,' he said, unashamedly taking Zola in.

Zola looked down at the food, pretending to be enthralled by the ingredients of the salad as she opened the plastic container.

'This is great. Thank you,' she mumbled, suddenly very conscious of how to hold a fork, how wide to open her mouth and how long it took to chew each mouthful.

Mbali seemed relaxed in her company, smiling and casually asking questions as if they were new friends and not virtual strangers who'd only met once, during a horrible meeting that hadn't even lasted five minutes.

'Tell me what lunch you like so I can be sure I get it right next time,' Mbali pressed.

Zola's nerves prevented her from telling him he should never come to her place of work. Instead, she made up a sophisticated list with which to impress Mbali.

'My favourites depend on the day, really. Salad today, sushi tomorrow ... I really love a good poke bowl,' she lied.

'And pizza? Burgers? Kota?' Mbali laughed. 'Come on, Zola – you guys are missing out on some really good food with all these weird diets of yours.'

Zola laughed too, and touched his arm but withdrew it immediately, not wanting to seem too forward.

'You know, I'm still wondering what they put in these salads,' Mbali said. 'I had to arm wrestle a girl for these.' He dramatically re-enacted the fight. 'I had the salad in my hands, and I was about to put it in the trolley when she pounced and grabbed it. I'm telling you, I did something I'm not proud of. But I thought your need for salad was greater than hers.'

'You're such a liar,' Zola laughed. 'Good-looking men like you tell such ugly lies.'

'Good-looking?' Mbali raised an eyebrow.

There was an awkward silence, and Zola looked down to spear her salad with a fork. Suddenly, the air was so charged that Zola could almost hear it ringing in her ears.

'Listen, I need to get back to the office, so I should go.' Mbali stood up, reached into the bag and pulled out a pack of cupcakes. 'But this has been great. And you can think of me when you have dessert.' He winked.

Bundling her leftover salad, the cooldrink and cupcakes into the shopping bag Mbali was holding open for her, Zola suddenly found herself in his arms, embraced in a warm hug she never saw coming.

There was no time to make sense of it before the angry growl of a car engine nearby sent Zola into a blind panic. She jumped out of Mbali's arms, feeling immediately guilty.

Okuhle's yellow Mustang drove past them, and even through the dark windscreen, Zola knew Okuhle was staring daggers at her.

The joy she had felt just moments ago was replaced by dread.

There was the beep of a car being locked and then the unmistakable clicking of Okuhle's heels.

'So *this* is what happens when I'm not around?' Okuhle's loud voice was tinged with something Zola couldn't place. 'Hello, Mbali.' She walked, beaming, towards Mbali, her arms spread open.

'Yes, Okuhle. When you aren't around, your worker bees actually take their lunch breaks,' Mbali said, hugging Okuhle fondly. 'And I was just leaving. Zola, I'll call you.' He winked at Zola before sliding into his car.

'It's a Chevrolet Corvette,' Zola whispered to herself as Mbali's taillights flashed their goodbye.

Chapter 12

Really bad vibes

Okuhle walked through reception and headed straight to her office without so much as a greeting to her staff. She shut the door behind her, glad to be away from Zola and whatever grovelling explanations she was preparing.

The bouquet on her desk made her sick. The flowers, their smell – it filled her office to suffocation. Okuhle opened the windows and then went to close the interior blinds to shut out the rest of her office. And then she saw it: the king-sized bouquet on Zola's desk, bigger, brighter and fresher than her one.

Mbali couldn't seriously be doing this to her. Was this one of his sick games, something to get back at her? Like the time he'd thrown her in the swimming pool? He probably just thought it was funny. She would need to tell him it was not.

Okuhle took one last look at Zola, still looking so innocent and fresh-faced despite her betrayal. Okuhle could see that Zola was working diligently and from the number of emails she had already CC'ed her in, it seemed she was doing a fantastic job.

'She just has to be good at everything, doesn't she?' Okuhle said bitterly to herself before shutting the blinds.

She sat down, pulled out her laptop and switched it on. And what do you know? More emails from Zola – updates on her to-do list, confirmations and details, all perfectly presented.

Zola really was amazing at her job, Okuhle thought. Only her second day and it looked like she could run this whole show on her own. But what was she doing with Mbali? The little bench in the car park used to be *their* spot. Mbali would bring her lunch while she stressed and agonised over starting her own company. It felt like a lifetime ago.

Okuhle tried to banish the memories. She busied herself with work, calling suppliers and creating mock-ups for marketing until hours later when she noticed the sun was setting.

She'd been so wrapped up in her own drama and trying to avoid Zola that she hadn't called the impromptu meeting she had come all the way back to the office for. Now people were leaving, and it would have to wait until tomorrow.

A soft knock on the door broke her thoughts. Okuhle was quiet, hoping whoever it was would assume she was busy and leave her alone.

'Okuhle?' Zola said, knocking softly at the door again.

Okuhle sat still and waited for Zola to give up and leave. But she didn't.

Zola opened the door a little and peeked through.

'Okuhle?' she whispered.

'Yes,' Okuhle turned, a smile painfully plastered over her face.

'I just wanted to let you know that I'm leaving now,' Zola said softly. She looked past Okuhle to a painting on the wall of a bluey-black woman with a halo of woolly hair made of rainbow-coloured raindrops. It kind of looked like Okuhle, but Zola couldn't be sure.

'Okay, safe journey!' Okuhle said in a sing-song voice. 'You did really well today.'

'Thank you,' Zola said. 'And … Okuhle? I only went outside for my lunch break, not any longer,' she added, a defence she felt was warranted since Okuhle hadn't spoken to her after her snide remark outside.

'What?' Okuhle stood up, walked towards the door and ushered Zola in. 'You thought I was serious? Oh, Zola, no,' Okuhle cooed.

Zola looked out of the window. She really wanted to leave on time today; the last thing she needed was another heart-to-heart with Okuhle. But she came in and sat across from Okuhle at her desk.

'I really hope you don't think I could be that unprofessional,' Okuhle said with a note of sadness.

Zola sighed. 'I just meant … in case that was what you thought. I didn't invite him here.' Her voice had an edge neither she nor Okuhle expected, but both decided it was fitting.

They were both quiet, Zola struggling not to pout and Okuhle doing all she could to keep her feelings in check.

She really didn't want to be angry at Zola, it wasn't her fault Mbali had chosen her for this twisted joke. In the end, Zola was more of a victim than she was – of that Okuhle was sure. She couldn't think of a single thing Mbali and Zola had in common. And even though Zola was nice enough, she wasn't Mbali's type.

'Of course you didn't.' Okuhle smiled sympathetically. 'Mbali is like that, overbearing. The flowers, the grand gestures …'

Okuhle realised she was wistfully listing all of Mbali's flaws and finding they were the things she liked most about being with him.

Zola glanced out of the window again. It was getting dark and Okuhle appeared to be gearing up for another long talk – the kind of talk she should be having with her friends, not with her brand-new employee. Maybe Okuhle didn't have many friends.

Zola realised with a pang that she didn't either.

Okuhle dreamily bit the end of her pen. 'He really is a charmer … Are you into him?' She snapped so quickly out of her daze that Zola jumped.

'*Into* him?'

'Yes. I mean, he obviously isn't doing this for nothing. He's obviously trying to get some sort of reaction from you. He *wants* something.' Having to explain this to Zola left a bitter taste in Okuhle's mouth.

Zola stared blankly at Okuhle. It made sense, and she understood exactly what Okuhle was saying – she just hadn't thought of it that way. She hadn't imagined that she had made that kind of impression on Mbali, and she definitely hadn't imagined that he'd be interested in her. Not like *that*, anyway.

'Well, he hasn't said anything about that to me,' Zola said. It was becoming increasingly clear that something didn't add up. Okuhle was too interested in her interactions with Mbali. Just seeing his name on a card had thrown her into a mood, and seeing him today had resulted in her giving the entire office the silent treatment. She was being weird. If there was a bad vibe in the office, Okuhle was the one who had brought it.

'Maybe he's trying to lure you in.' Okuhle winked suggestively. 'You did say you're single, right?'

Zola was clearly not as pliable as Okuhle had first thought. Okuhle had always surrounded herself with people who wanted her opinion on things and simply adopted it in place of their own. But Zola didn't seem that much affected by her. Maybe she liked Mbali, maybe she was charmed by his attention, mesmerised by his flashy car.

'Anyway, I wasn't trying to convince you of anything. I was just telling you what I know about him, one girl to another,' Okuhle said ruefully.

Zola stood up to leave. 'I have to go – it's getting late.'

This time Okuhle didn't offer to walk her to the door, and she didn't even stand up. Something had changed, and they both had a pretty good idea what it was.

Zola walked out of the office into the dark, her mind racing, and she hardly looked up from the ground until she'd reached the main road and got on her first taxi into the Johannesburg CBD. She looked out the window as her view changed from lush greenery shimmering under streetlights to the highway, quieter now that it was late evening. The taxi drove through an old suburb and then through the dingy streets of Joburg, past overburdened blocks of flats with clothing hanging on the balconies. Zola felt the change before she even saw it. Her body tensed automatically; she didn't trust the window not to slide open in the dark and for some stranger's arm to fly in and grab her bag off her lap.

Zola climbed out of the taxi at its last stop and half-ran down the street to the next taxi rank. Running was not a prerequisite – in fact, most people just walked briskly, dodging cars and people, making sure to walk as close to the street as possible when passing an alleyway. Zola wasn't street smart, she'd never thought she'd need to be, and she was already plotting how never to be in this position again.

She caught her taxi and squeezed her way to the back. Squashed from both sides and trying to catch her breath, it was hard not to blame Okuhle for all of this. Okuhle was probably home by now, lighting incense, drinking wine and playing jazz. She seemed the type.

Zola had known from the moment she'd seen Okuhle with Mbali that there was much more to them just growing up around each other. As Zola was jostled about in the back of the taxi – the smell of one stranger's breath, another's dinner and another's sweat all mingling in her nose – it seemed obvious that Okuhle had been playing her, manipulating her. Okuhle saw her as a threat.

Zola from Vosloo was a threat to the glamorous Okuhle Msimanga.

'Ma, I'm telling you, I didn't do anything to her,' Zola protested at the dinner table.

Her mother shook her head in disbelief.

'Your boss asked you to stay away from that boy, and you think you're smart now because he's giving you a little attention?' Nomsebenzi scooped cabbage onto the papa she was holding with the tips of her fingers.

Thobile laughed. 'No, Ma, but Okuhle is only Zola's boss at *work*.

THE THING WITH ZOLA

When it comes to her personal life, Okuhle must back off. I mean, the guy is clearly into Zola. The flowers, the lunch … Zola! And here you were thinking your life was over when Günter dumped you!'

Zola flinched at the mention of his name – she'd somehow managed to stop thinking about their last conversation. When she'd had nothing else to look forward to, she'd always hoped it was him when her phone rang or when she got a message – though it was usually someone trying to sell her something, or offering her a loan. Each time, she'd let her irritation rain down on the poor caller, who hadn't known what had hit them.

'He didn't dump me,' Zola mumbled. 'It was just a disagreement.'

For weeks now, Zola had been convinced of that. And she'd waited for him to call, text, email, anything to apologise … but the longer he kept quiet, the more final everything seemed.

Clearly he owed her an apology. He'd been in the wrong and it wasn't for her to go crawling back – though maybe it wouldn't be so bad to let him know he *could* still come back, that she'd accept his apology if he offered it.

When the dishes were washed, her outfit for the next day was pressed and she was lying in her bed, her mother snoring from the other room and her sister breathing in the bed next to hers, Zola scrolled through her phone looking at photos …

Pictures of Günter, of her and Günter, of her taken by Günter …

She felt robbed.

She hadn't looked for love in Germany and yet she'd found it even before she'd started her first class. Surely that was fate, destiny?

Something she couldn't let go of just because they were going through a rough patch?

Chapter 13

Something about Zola

There was something about Zola that made it impossible for Okuhle to blame her for what was going on, even though it would be so much easier to hate her than to face the truth about Mbali.

On her drive home, Okuhle phoned her mother to explain the situation. Maybe it was time for both their families to sit down and tell Mbali that it was time to settle.

'Oh, baby, it's so hard for me to watch you go through this,' said her mother, Priscilla. 'You know your father and I would do anything to make you happy, but our hands are tied. You don't think maybe it's time you moved on too?'

Okuhle felt the tears burning behind her eyes. It had been her mother along with Mbali's who had advised she wait for him. They knew men, they'd assured her, and Mbali would, like his father, appreciate a patient woman.

'Mom, you said he'd come around,' Okuhle sobbed.

THE THING WITH ZOLA

Her mother was quiet and Okuhle knew it wasn't because of a bad line – she could still hear her mother's favourite soapie blaring in the background.

'I don't know what to tell you,' Priscilla said after a long and thoughtful pause. 'Mbali is an idiot, and you deserve better. As for that skank at your office, you need to get rid of that girl – she sounds like trouble, tsk!' Priscilla clicked her tongue, dragging the sound as long as her breath would allow.

Okuhle sniffed. Yes, Mbali was an idiot – the games he was playing were beyond hurtful – but he was *her* idiot. He was supposed to have come back to her full of regret having realised it had been her all along – that she was the one.

It was obvious to Okuhle that Zola was just a pawn in Mbali's game – she couldn't be anything more. Okuhle had wracked her brain for why Mbali had chosen Zola, but the only thing she could think of was that Zola worked for her.

Still, Okuhle had known that her mother would blame Zola – that was her style.

'It's really not Zola's fault, Mom – she doesn't even know Mbali all that well. *He's* the one pursuing *her*,' Okuhle explained. 'She's great at her job, super-smart and way overqualified – I'd be stupid to let her go. Besides, Mom, we don't blame women for men's failings any more,' she sanctimoniously reminded her mother as she pulled into her complex, drove towards her townhouse and parked outside.

The lights were off. Of course there was no one home, and no one would be coming home. She was alone, as usual, and she was sick of it.

'Well, then, Okuhle, maybe you need to leave the Thabethe boy alone. I know you've had your heart set on him, but, baby, there are so many better men out there. Men who won't play games, and who won't make your father and I wait so long for those cows.' Priscilla gave a long, drawn-out sigh. 'Besides, if you're set on being Mrs Mbali Thabethe, you should probably get used to his … indiscretions,' she muttered through clenched teeth. Priscilla was the master of the audible whisper, and every time she did it Okuhle knew her mother was about to spill the tea.

'What are you talking about, Mom?' Secretly, Okuhle loved hearing about all the scandalous things her mother's friends got up to. 'Do you have gossip again?'

Priscilla laughed. 'Ongama is in Bali again for a retreat – so I think you know what I mean ...'

So Mbali's mother was in Bali recovering from one of her husband's many adulterous affairs. Okuhle wasn't surprised – this had happened more than once before.

'That woman should consider getting a combination lock for her husband,' Okuhle said firmly. 'Sooner or later he's going to catch something that a trip to Bali won't fix.'

Okuhle knew the Thabethes were far from perfect, but they hid it well. From the outside, they were the picture of black love, black excellence and morality. In reality, they were more chaotic than most families and all the money in the world couldn't make them truly happy.

It was a picture she chose to ignore when she thought about her life with Mbali. She had proved that she could fix most things, so she was sure she could fix him too – and that nothing would stand in the way of their perfect future.

'Like you, Ongama doesn't know when to give up,' Priscilla said seriously. 'Next week, you and I will go to the black business convention, where I'm sure you'll meet many amazing and successful men ... Anyway, baby, I must go.'

Hanging up wouldn't make walking into her home any easier, but Okuhle said her goodbyes, climbed out of the car and headed into her dark, lonely house.

Walking in, she didn't even bother turning on the lights. Instead, she headed straight for the fridge and used its open-door light to find a large wineglass.

She hadn't eaten, but what the hell – she had no appetite anyway. She gulped down her first glass of wine and poured herself a second. Then she wandered to the couch and sat there blinking into the darkness.

'Who does he think he is?' Okuhle whispered to herself as she took another long sip. 'Seriously, what makes him think he can walk all over me like this?'

After draining her second glass she went to pour herself another, and after a generous sip decided it was time to call Mbali and give him a piece of her mind.

She rummaged through her bag to find her phone and dialled his number. As it rang and rang, it occurred to her that she needed to urinate, so she staggered upstairs, wineglass in hand. Just when she thought the call was about to go to voicemail, Mbali answered.

'Hey, Okuhle, what's up?'

'What's *up*? *That's* what you say to me? What's *up*?'

Clearly irritated, Mbali sighed deeply and loudly. 'Okay … What's the problem, Okuhle?'

Okuhle breathed into the phone and felt desperation rise in her. She was dimly aware that the wine had hit her faster than she'd expected, but even she was surprised by the force of the sob that erupted from her.

'But *why*, Mbali?' she wailed. 'Why won't you jusht shee me …?' Now in the bathroom, she tried unsuccessfully to muffle the sound of her tinkling on the loo.

Mbali couldn't mask his amusement. 'Okuhle, are you in the *toilet*?'

'Sho what if I'm in the toilet? Sho what? Do you think Zola doeshn't ushe the toilet? Becaushe I can tell you …. she doesh.'

Okuhle flushed, drained her glass and left it on a side table at the top of the stairs so she could hold the banister with both hands on the way down.

'You're clearly drunk, Okuhle. Where are you?' Mbali asked, a hint of laughter still in his voice.

'I'm at home,' Okuhle said taking a cautious step. 'Alone. In my three-bedroomed townhouse, in a pet-friendly complex with a lovely shwimming pool and kiddies' playgroundsh.' Okuhle sobbed. She missed a step but recovered with the help of the banister.

'You could always move. Get one of those serviced hotel apartments close to your office, the mall, good restaurants ...' Mbali soothed, his voice earnest.

'*What*? Is that sheriously all you can shay? After all these yearsh I've waited for you ...' Okuhle was sobbing openly now.

'Come on, man, don't do this, Okuhle,' Mbali whined. 'Things didn't work out. I didn't ask you to wait around for me. You could have moved on. You *should* have moved on.'

Okuhle cried loudly. 'Okay, fine! Mbali, if you say so, I'll just – aaaaaah!' With one badly placed step she went tumbling down the stairs, her phone still in her hand.

'Okuhle? What's going on there?'

Okuhle's crying was no longer drunken sobbing – it sounded like she was in pain.

'Mbali, please help me,' Okuhle croaked.

'Okay, okay, hang in there, Okuhle. I'll send an ambulance – it'll reach you faster than I can.'

'Awwwwwww! I think my arm is broken,' Okuhle cried. 'No, not an ambulance. *You* come. And please don't hang up, Mbali. Please, baby ...'

'Okay, stay calm. I'm on my way. Hey, Okuhle – do you remember that time we climbed into my gran's apple tree and you were too afraid to climb down?'

Okuhle grunted petulantly. 'I was ten.'

'Yeah, but you're still always getting yourself into situations you can't get out of,' Mbali chuckled.

Her fall seemed to have had a sobering effect because Okuhle had quickly recovered her senses. Over the phone, she could hear his car door slam shut, the beeping sound warning him to put on his seatbelt and then the roar of the powerful engine.

'Not always – you're exaggerating. That was just one time,' Okuhle said, gritting her teeth through the pain in her arm.

'Not only once. You remember that school trip to the waterpark? You climbed all the way to the top of the highest slide, but then you were too scared to come down on your own. Do you remember how much you cried?'

'I do remember that. And I also remember that you climbed up that apple tree, and carried me down on your back.' Okuhle gritted her teeth and smiled at the memory. 'And at the waterpark you pushed your way to the front of the line so you could hold me as we went down the slide together …'

'You're sounding a lot more sober now,' Mbali observed.

Okuhle sighed. 'Falling down the stairs will do that to you.'

'It's okay. I'm on my way. I've got you.'

Chapter 14

Clarity

Her first weekend after starting her new job; Zola peeked out from the top of her covers and saw her sister still asleep. The sun streamed in through their bedroom window. Nomsebenzi had already left for work.

Zola sighed and rolled over to stare at the ceiling. She had nowhere to go, nothing to do, but even though she'd only had a job for a few days, she was glad for the break.

'Thobile?' Zola whispered.

'Hmmmmm?' Thobile groaned.

'Do you think I should call Günter?'

Thobile nearly fell over as she rolled over in her small bed. '*Now?*' she asked squinting at Zola.

Zola sighed. 'Maybe I overreacted. I shouldn't have been so dramatic about him having people over. It's not like it's my place – and I don't even live there any more.'

Thobile stood up and stretched. 'Sounds like you already know and you've made up your mind. I'm going to go watch TV.'

Zola sat up and took a few deep breaths before she dialled Günter's number. The phone rang unanswered and then went to voicemail. Was he avoiding her? Maybe it really was over.

Zola got up and decided to have a bath, filling the tub more than she could when her mother was home and pouring in a large glug of bubble bath. She lay in the tub consoling herself: it wasn't like she was going to see him again anyway ... she was already overextending herself ... *he* was the one who should have called to apologise ... she was better off without him ...

When her phone rang in the bedroom, Zola sprang from the bath, covered in suds, and slipped and slid her way to the bedroom, slamming the door behind her and answering without even looking at the screen.

'Hello?' she said, trying to sound cool and calm.

'Hi, Zola!' Okuhle's preppy voice rang through the phone. 'I'm sorry to bother you on the weekend – I know how important work-life balance is!' She sounded like an infomercial, and it grated.

'Okuhle,' Zola sighed. She just couldn't seem to get away from this woman, and while it was Okuhle's bubbly personality and overbearing friendliness that had convinced Zola that she would be the perfect boss, right now Zola just wanted to be left alone.

'I've had an accident,' Okuhle announced, somewhat triumphantly. 'My collarbone is broken and my wrist is sprained, but I'll survive.'

'I'm sorry to hear it,' Zola said and waited for why this had anything to do with her on a Saturday morning.

'Thank you,' Okuhle said, and then paused as if waiting for more sympathy.

None came – Zola was too occupied with her own drama.

'Um, I was hoping you could do me a favour,' Okuhle said, her voice whiney and high-pitched. 'You know how important the African Wedding Expo is to me?' she started to explain. 'I need to work today if we're going to meet our deadlines. Could you come to the hospital to help me a little? We'll bill it as overtime.'

Zola sighed and felt the joy drain from her body. So much for the weekend.

'Okay, send me your location,' Zola said, already trying to figure out how she'd get there.

'I'll send an Uber to come get you,' Okuhle said. She sounded almost excited, which irritated Zola even more. If she had been a little less keen to talk to Günter she could have missed Okuhle's call altogether.

But Zola was rarely lucky.

An hour later, laptop in hand, Zola waved sadly at Thobile as she climbed into the Uber and headed to a secluded private clinic in Muldersdrift. Once there, Zola marvelled at the beautiful green gardens – this looked more like a boutique hotel than a clinic or hospital.

She followed a nurse to Okuhle's room. Just as she'd suspected, there were no white walls and blue floors here. Instead, the private bedroom's windows opened straight onto the garden. Okuhle practically had a living room in here, complete with big-screen TV. And she was sitting on the couch eating popcorn.

'This doesn't look much like a hospital,' Zola said.

'I know, right!' Okuhle smiled. 'It's a recovery centre. I live alone, so this is the best option for me while I can't use my arm.'

'Oh. You couldn't go home to your parents?'

Okuhle shrugged. 'They're hardly ever home. Between their work and their social lives, they wouldn't be able to help me much, and I don't want to burden them.' She made room for Zola on the couch.

Zola's heart sank. She'd already guessed that Okuhle didn't have many friends – her boss had opened up to Zola so immediately it seemed unlikely that she had a posse of girlfriends waiting in the wings for wine and daily downloads. But it was sad that she didn't even have anyone she could depend on while she was recovering. Obviously, Okuhle's parents could do things for her that Nomsebenzi couldn't do for Zola, but at least Zola could be sure that if she'd broken her collarbone, her mother would bend over backwards to care for her. She felt a bit sorry for Okuhle, actually.

And I wonder what happened? Zola thought, curiously. How had this poor little rich girl ended up in a five-star hospital with no one to look after her?

Zola sat down next to Okuhle and looked at her.

'So, what happened?' Zola asked.

It was clear Okuhle liked the attention. 'Oh, the lights were off at my place and I fell down the stairs,' she said, leaving out the bit about the wine and being on the phone to their mutual 'friend', Mbali.

'I'm so sorry. That must have been so painful,' Zola said sincerely.

'So the thing is, I need to send out some emails and I can't use my hands. I thought of you since you already know pretty much everything that's going on and you could probably help with other things ... I'm probably not thinking quite straight.' Okuhle smiled sweetly.

'Of course.' Zola switched on her laptop and fetched Okuhle's from one of the bedroom's numerous cupboards. She noticed that Okuhle's wardrobe had been carefully stocked with her personal items as well as snacks and treats from some high-end stores. *Someone* must care about her.

Zola had just sat back down when her cellphone rang with a video call. As it happened, Okuhle had a clear view of the screen before Zola could grab it.

'*Günter?*' Okuhle teased, passing Zola the phone. 'He's cute.'

Zola gave her a thin smile and answered before hurriedly retreating to the corridor.

'Hi.' Zola smiled and waved at the phone.

'Hey,' Günter said smiling back. 'Everything okay?'

'Yeah ... why?' Her happiness at seeing him quickly dissolved into defensiveness. 'Why shouldn't it be?'

Günter shook his head and sighed, blowing his breath into a lock of hair that had dangled down over his forehead.

'Because you're in a hospital, Zola,' he said, then nervously pushed his hair back with his hand. 'I checked your location before I called.'

Stupid app. Zola sighed, leant against the wall and let herself slide down until she was sitting on the plush carpeted floor a little way from Okuhle's suite.

'I'm sorry. I'm just ... I don't know how to talk to you any more,' Zola admitted. 'I don't even know if you want to talk to me.'

Günter looked down guiltily. 'I'm also sorry, Zo. I've taken your leaving very badly. I know you tried to stay here and that you're trying to come back home to me. But most of the time the only thing that matters is that you aren't here right now.'

It had taken Zola a while to get used to it, but now she loved it when Günter got all emotional. At least she knew what he was thinking when he poured out his heart.

'Not like my jealous rages were any better,' Zola admitted, getting up off the floor and walking a little further down the corridor. 'And I'm totally fine – I'm just visiting my new boss in this hospital. Honestly, Günter, this place is supposed to be some sort of recovery clinic, but I swear it's a hotel.' Zola laughed and then dropped her voice. 'My boss fell and broke her collarbone.'

Zola was swinging her phone around for Günter to see when Okuhle opened the door and waved. 'Ah, Zola – don't forget me!' she called jokingly.

Zola flared her nostrils for Günter's benefit – a small gesture that reminded them both of how things used to be. The silent conversations, the looks and smiles and winks that spoke whole paragraphs.

'Don't hang up, I want to see the room,' Günter said as Zola walked back.

'Yeah, don't hang up. I want to meet the boyfriend,' Okuhle cheered.

Chapter 15

Musical chairs

Cringing, Zola continued with Günter's tour into Okuhle's room.

'Show him the view!' Okuhle squealed. 'Oh, and these cute cushions! Has he seen the bathroom? Show him that …'

Zola walked around the room with constant commentary from Okuhle, who seemed to be falling over herself to be friendly to Günter.

'So, Günter, how has the long distance been treating you?' Okuhle asked. 'You coping without your Zola?'

'Yes, only just.' Günter shrugged. As much as he had opened his heart to Zola, she knew he wasn't likely to confess his feelings to a stranger. Zola read his crossed eyebrows as confused irritation – it was clear he wanted out of the side conversation with Okuhle, and the more she talked, the worse it got.

'Maybe you should consider coming to South Africa since Zola probably won't be able to get back to Germany,' Okuhle continued, oblivious or not – Zola wasn't sure.

Zola's eyes became wider. She had never spoken to Okuhle about trying to get back to Germany and she hadn't even mentioned Günter. But from this conversation it sounded like Okuhle knew everything about her life and circumstances.

'Maybe I should,' Günter said. That was news to Zola, and she couldn't tell if he was serious. She really, *really* wanted to have a proper conversation with him, just the two of them.

'When you decide, let me know. I don't like to brag, but I'm kind of connected.' Okuhle actually winked at him.

Zola knew it wasn't a joke – Okuhle really was connected and maybe she could help – but she didn't want her to be that involved.

'Err, let me show you the bathroom,' Zola said, disappearing from Okuhle's sight and hopefully out of earshot.

'Do you think she could help me get settled that side?' Günter asked seriously.

Zola raised an eyebrow. 'You've never mentioned wanting to come here. I didn't know that was even an option.'

'I just want to be wherever you are,' Günter said.

Zola felt her knees go weak and hastily sat down on the closed toilet. She couldn't believe she and Günter had gone days without talking to each other over something they'd both gotten over literally in seconds.

'I should get back to Okuhle and my work. And yes, I know it's Saturday.' Zola made a dramatic sad face.

Günter played at crying. 'I'll talk to you again tonight. I love you, Zo.'

'I love you too.'

Zola smiled. Her heart felt like it was flowing over the brim. She took a moment to enjoy the feeling before opening the bathroom door and returning to Okuhle, who probably had a long list of questions about Günter, their relationship and only she knew what else. It was going to be a long day.

But as Zola walked back into the room, the first person she saw was Mbali carefully packing Okuhle's closet.

Where had *he* come from?

'Hi,' Zola said awkwardly.

Mbali smiled with equal awkwardness. 'Oh, hey, Zola. I didn't know you were here.'

'Yeah, Zola's been here a while, but we haven't gotten anything done yet because she's been busy talking to her *boyfriend*,' Okuhle piped. Zola was sure she heard an unnatural emphasis on the last word.

'It's really sweet,' Okuhle continued. 'I mean, the fact that they've kept it going with the long-distance thing – so romantic. And there's no way *I'm* going to stand in the way of love!'

No one responded, but on she went: 'Anyway, I really think it would be easier for Günter to come down to South Africa – it would be a lot easier than Zola trying to get back into Germany. You think your dad could help, Mbali?'

He was done packing the closet and was just standing there listening as Okuhle prattled on, his eyes a bit wider than usual, Zola thought.

'Err, I don't know if Günter actually *wants* to come here. We'd need to talk about that,' Zola said, desperate for a change in subject. 'I'm sorry, I've really wasted your time. Can we get started with the work now?'

Okuhle nodded and settled down on the couch as Zola opened Okuhle's emails.

'Okay, so who are we emailing?' Zola asked.

'Sorry, sorry, I'm still distracted. I just can't *believe* you didn't tell me about Günter!' Okuhle gushed.

Zola sighed and sank further into the couch.

'Oh my word, Zola – you know this would be a great angle for the expo, don't you think? How intercontinental marriages work …? We should definitely include something like that …'

Zola nodded, waiting impatiently for Okuhle to tell her what she actually needed help with, what was so urgent that Zola had had to come all this way on a Saturday? So she was relieved when Okuhle's interest in Günter finally seemed to run out of steam.

'Okay, right, let's get to work. Mbali, are you okay there?' Okuhle asked. 'Not too bored?'

From where he was now sitting on Okuhle's bed, Mbali shook his head and continued scrolling through his phone.

For the next few hours, Okuhle dictated and Zola typed. Every now and again Zola suggested a detail that clearly impressed Okuhle, which sent their conversation veering off in another direction. But they had managed to get a lot of work done by the time it was dark outside. It was Mbali who broke the productivity spell.

'Ladies, I can't let you go on like this on a Saturday. Hlehle, you've done Zola wrong – you haven't even given her anything to eat!' He sprang up from the bed, strode across the room and snapped shut Okuhle's laptop, much to Zola's relief.

Okuhle picked up her cellphone to check the time. 'Oh flip, let me get you both some dinner. We can all eat together before you leave, Zola.'

Zola was about to object – she seriously wanted to go home – but Mbali shook his head.

'Rest time for you, Hlehle,' he admonished. 'How are you going to heal when you don't eat and you don't rest?'

Okuhle blushed with pleasure at his affectionate scolding and pouted for Zola's benefit.

'You're right. Zola, you're a trooper, thank you.' Okuhle reached over to hug Zola. 'Let me get you a ride home.'

'It's fine,' Mbali cut in and swiftly picked up Zola's bags. 'I'll take Zola home. I was thinking of getting iskopo anyway.'

'Seriously? You're going to go all the way to Vosloo for *sheep's head*?' Okuhle's normally happy face looked grim. 'That's almost an hour away.'

'And it's where they make the best skopo,' Mbali said. 'I'll check on you later, Hlehle.' And without a moment's hesitation he led Zola out of the room.

Okuhle stood at the door and watched Mbali and Zola walk away together laughing and joking. Things had backfired, she knew that, but somehow the thought of Günter pining for Zola almost thirteen thousand kilometres away made her feel better.

Chapter 16

Road trip

'I didn't know Vosloo was known for iskopo,' Zola said, looking at Mbali suspiciously as they emerged into the hospital parking lot.

Mbali laughed. 'Neither did I, but who knows how long you'd have been in there if I hadn't said anything.'

Zola knew Mbali was right. Being in that room with Okuhle had felt something like a hostage situation, but while she hadn't had much choice, Mbali had spent the day there voluntarily. There was clearly something she didn't know about Okuhle and Mbali. And right now, she didn't want to know. All Zola wanted was to be at home, to call Günter and to fall asleep dreaming she was back in his arms.

'So, you have a boyfriend?' Mbali smiled as he opened the Chevrolet's door for Zola.

'Mhm.' She nodded and gave him a thin-lipped smile. The hour's drive from Muldersdrift to Vosloorus was going to be seriously awkward.

'A white guy?' Mbali said climbing into the driver seat and adjusting his seat to be further back than Zola thought could possibly be comfortable.

'Is there something wrong with dating a white guy?' Zola asked defensively. 'I wasn't aware we had slipped back into apartheid,' she said staring out of the window.

Being in a taxi with a stranger or even sixteen strangers would be better than this, she decided. At least she wouldn't feel like she was being interrogated, especially not by someone who had his own questions to answer.

As they drove, Zola watched the green hills in the distance – hotels and resorts scattered at the ends of dusty roads, markings for hiking trails and the Cradle of Humankind a short distance away.

'Did you also go on those lame school trips to the Cradle of Humankind?' Mbali asked, carefully choosing an easier topic of conversation.

'Who didn't? We took the ugliest, oldest bus there and it smelt of hot chips, fried chicken, stew and sweat. Worst school trip of my life.'

Mbali shrugged. 'Stinky bus rides are some of my favourite memories of school.' He looked over at Zola. 'Waking up really early to get to the bus on time, the rush, the excitement. I miss those days.'

Zola didn't need to know, but she was curious and she couldn't think of a subtler segue: 'I can't imagine Okuhle in a bus full of sweaty teens.'

Mbali didn't hesitate or flinch. 'Neither can I.'

'I thought you went to school together?' Zola asked. She was sure that's what Okuhle had said.

'Oh, we did,' Mbali said, slowing down the car and pulling into a rest stop. 'But let's just say Okuhle's parents were more hands-on than most.'

As soon as they had come to a stop he unclicked his seatbelt and climbed out of his seat.

Confused, Zola sat for a moment. Mbali hadn't even bothered to tell her why they were stopping, but he'd walked around to her side of the car and opened the door for her.

'Um, why are we here?'

Even though she didn't think Mbali was a likely suspect, she'd heard about all kinds of disappearances from remote places like this.

'Zola, you haven't had a meal all day. Let's get something to eat,' he said casually.

Zola climbed out of the car and saw a small retro-looking restaurant up ahead. Within moments of them walking to it, a small group of people had gathered around Mbali's car to take pictures. He was obviously used to it, and didn't bat an eyelid.

'What do you mean Okuhle's parents were hands-on?' Zola asked, sliding into the fifties-diner-styled cubicle.

Mbali pouted and exhaled a silent whistle. 'I mean they wouldn't let her drive in the bus with the rest of us – even though it was a luxury coach. Her mother sent her ahead with a driver.'

Now *that* Zola could imagine. Even with her whole chakra-queen image, Okuhle was definitely a pampered princess used to getting her own way.

'Wow.' Zola picked up the sticky menu and looked through it. 'The other half really do live in a different world.'

Mbali sighed. 'Different doesn't always mean easy.'

Zola sensed that he was oddly protective of Okuhle. Even though he criticised her, he took offence to Zola doing it.

'I'm not too sure about that,' she persisted. 'Having a personal driver sounds a lot easier than having to navigate through life in a taxi. In my opinion, Okuhle had it made from the beginning.'

Without looking up from his menu, Mbali raised a hand to call over a waiter.

'But look how she turned out,' he said, and then glanced across at Zola. 'Please don't order a salad. I hate how some women pretend they don't eat.'

Zola pursed her lips. She'd been looking forward to a burger, but for a moment she considered ordering the salad just to spite him.

'Let's call it a cheat day,' he said, and ordered himself a burger and chips.

Zola ordered the same, along with a milkshake.

'A girl with an appetite. Hans is a lucky man.'

'His name is Günter,' Zola snapped.

She and Günter had just made up – the last thing she needed was this stranger poking holes in their relationship.

'Sorry. Günter. Do you think Günter would survive life in the African wild?'

It wasn't the question that irritated Zola – she'd wondered if he'd be able to live here herself. It was Mbali's tone. He was sizing Günter up in absentia, and she didn't like it.

'He'd be fine,' she said, and pulled out her phone so she wouldn't have to continue the conversation.

'How long have you two been together?' Mbali persisted.

It was like an interview, only they were in the middle of nowhere and Mbali was her only ride home. She was stuck.

'Oh, a long time,' she said vaguely.

'And how long do you plan on staying together?' Mbali raised a brow.

Zola narrowed her eyes and clicked her tongue. 'That really isn't something you should ask someone you barely know.'

'How would I go about getting to know you if you won't talk to me?' Mbali continued. His intentions were clear enough and Zola could see right through him.

'Are you trying to get to know me, or are you trying to get to know my boyfriend? Because I could introduce you two,' Zola said, grateful that the waiter was returning with their food.

Zola pulled a pack of sanitising napkins out of her bag and handed one to Mbali. She wiped her own hands carefully and hoped to be able to eat in peace.

'Fine, then I'll ask questions about you. How's work?' he asked biting into his burger.

Zola paused before she spoke, reminding herself not to ever talk badly about her boss. The last thing she needed was to start job-hunting again. Besides, she still had no idea of the nature of Mbali's relationship with Okuhle.

'It's something new and exciting, and I'm really grateful for the opportunity,' she said diplomatically.

Mbali laughed, his hands over his mouth. 'This isn't a job interview, Zola. You can speak like a normal person, you know!'

'This *is* how I speak. Besides, I'm not about to spill the tea to my boss's boyfriend. So this might as well be a job interview.'

She suspected her joke might be spiked with truth. It was the only reason Okuhle could have been so cagey about Mbali, why she was so upset about the flowers he'd sent and why Mbali had been the one bringing her everything she needed while she was at her fancy recovery hospital-cum-hotel.

With a nod, Mbali acknowledged Zola's attempt at prying. 'So why don't you just ask me?' he said.

'Ask you what?' Zola asked back, pretending not to understand.

'What you really want to know,' he said. 'Like why I was in Okuhle's room today.'

Zola twisted her lips around her straw and waited, but Mbali had been serious – he wanted her to ask.

'Okay, okay,' Zola tried to sound casual. 'Why were you in Okuhle's room today? Stocking up her clothes, bringing her snacks? That sounds like husband or at least boyfriend duties to me.'

Whatever Mbali's answer was, she knew things would be weird. Mbali was either Okuhle's boyfriend or he was trying to be hers.

'Okuhle is like a sister to me. Our parents are friends so we saw each other a lot growing up. Her parents are away at their house in Cape Town, so I came to help her out.' He raised his palms to show how simple the story was.

'Oh.' Zola suspected there was more to it.

'Look, I know Okuhle can be difficult. Sometimes she's a little much even for me, but she means well. It's just that—'

'She's had a difficult life?' Zola couldn't help finishing the sentence for him.

'Exactly. I know from the outside it looks like Okuhle has it made, that everything comes so easily for her. But it doesn't.'

'Go on,' said Zola between bites of her burger. She was genuinely interested in how a woman like Okuhle, who had everything she could ever possibly want, could be described as having a difficult life.

'Well, if the girl next door got a puppy, then Okuhle wanted five. If she woke up in Joburg and wanted to go to the beach, she'd have her toes in the sand by lunchtime,' Mbali described a charmed life with a sympathetic look that didn't match his words.

'Basically, she got everything she wanted and got used to having everything her way. And after a life like that, it's not easy to hear the word "no". It doesn't make it easy to make friends either,' Mbali said in a low voice that registered surprising sincerity.

They really were from two very different worlds, Zola realised. She might never actually comprehend the 'suffering' that Okuhle had been through, but she found Mbali's sudden sensitivity quite captivating.

'But now she's got *you*!' Zola exclaimed.

Mbali considered things for a moment.

'Yeah,' he said. 'She's got me.'

Chapter 17

What will the neighbours say?

An awkward silence descended on Zola and Mbali, as if talking about Okuhle had somehow conjured her right to the table. Zola found it difficult to even raise her eyes from her plate, and it seemed the feeling was mutual.

The silence followed them out the restaurant and back to the Chevrolet, where Mbali opened the door for Zola as if he didn't even see the excited children tearing away from their parents to pose in front of it.

Zola climbed in self-consciously and covered her face as Mbali revved the car's engine – to much cheering and whistling from outside. For the next forty minutes she switched between staring at her phone and looking out at the road ahead, wishing Mbali would turn on the radio or say something – she'd even stretch to talking about Günter at this point.

Mbali seemed to know where he was going. Confidently and without asking for directions he took various off-ramps and turns into streets

Zola didn't recognise, but after a little while she realised they were on the pothole-riddled road that led into Vosloorus.

'You can drop me off here – it's close to home,' Zola said after a particularly rough dip.

'It's dark already. I'll drop you off at your gate,' said Mbali.

'It's just …' Zola was suddenly flustered by the prospect of Mbali knowing where she lived. 'I don't want you ruining your car on the potholes.'

'Don't worry about it. The potholes aren't *your* fault. Just tell me where to turn.'

'Okay, it's left here.' She sighed and Mbali smiled at her.

'Hey, what's wrong?'

Zola ignored the question. 'And right here.'

They drove for another ten minutes before turning into Zola's street. A few metres down, Mbali parked his car right outside the chicken-wire fence outside her house.

A shame she didn't know she carried weighed heavily on her.

Before she could even open the car door, Zola noticed Ma'Liphotho from across the street peeking through her living-room window at the flashy Chevrolet. A small group of children stopped to admire the sports car, running their fingers over it as they passed by.

'Sorry,' Zola said.

'For what?' Mbali wearily stretched his arms towards the steering wheel.

'You've had to drive for hours to get me home, your tyres are getting worn down by our messed-up roads and now my little neighbours have probably scratched your car.'

'I've enjoyed getting to know you better,' Mbali said. The timbre of his voice dropped, and Zola knew exactly what that meant.

'Thank you for the ride!' she said airily, her hand on the door handle.

'Wait!' Mbali said. 'So, when can I see you again? Because I know you don't want me coming by your office or sending you any more flowers there.' He chuckled.

Zola blushed. Men like Mbali lived on the pages of novels she had read. She'd seen them on TV and in movies, but never in real life. He was confident, charismatic, over the top in all the right ways. It was like he knew he would always get things his way …

'No, I really don't like being the centre of office gossip,' Zola said intentionally meeting Mbali's stare.

'Ooh,' Mbali said, turning to face her. 'Tell me more.'

Relaxing a little, Zola let go of the door handle and turned back towards Mbali.

'It's not like anyone would actually tell me any of the gossip – I mean, I'm the new girl – but I know there were whispers after the first bouquet of flowers arrived, and on my first day too.' Zola covered her face with her palms. 'Then you had to come to the office – and that definitely got people talking.'

'That gossip really isn't as interesting as you made it out to be,' he said. 'You oversold, so now you owe me something genuinely interesting.'

Zola tried to hide a smile. 'I don't think I have anything interesting to tell you.'

'Oh yes, you do.' Mbali rubbed his hands together. 'That email you sent, was it meant to fend me off?'

Zola felt uncomfortable again. 'Yes,' she admitted. 'But in my defence, I didn't write it. I didn't even see it until after you'd called me about it.'

'I see.' Mbali sat back in his seat. 'And do you wish it had worked?' he asked, staring straight ahead of him out the windscreen.

Zola looked at him for a moment, taking him in. He was anxious – his tightened jaw made his temples pulse.

'No,' she said slowly. 'I'm glad it didn't work.'

'Zola!' Nomsebenzi shouted from the other side of the fence. Her arms were folded over her chest, her pink gown tied tightly around her ample waist. She looked livid. 'Hey! Zola!' she shouted again.

'I *definitely* have to go,' said Zola, picking up her bag and scurrying out of the car. 'Thank you so much for the ride.' She closed the door and hurried into the yard.

Mbali sat in the car for a moment and watched her walk through the gate. Then he drove off, revving the engine as he passed a group of guys sitting on the street corner, watching him.

'I don't know how you lived in Germany all those years, but in my house we lock the gate at seven,' her mother shouted as she led Zola back into the house.

'Mama, I'm not a child!' Zola shouted back, both irritated and embarrassed. What on earth would Mbali think?

'Now you are going to shout at me in my own house?' Nomsebenzi shrieked.

'Mama, don't shout,' Zola said lowering her voice. 'I was just outside.'

Nomsebenzi grabbed a glass and filled it with water, her hands shaking. 'Ma'Liphotho sent me a message telling me you were in some sugar daddy's car doing God-knows-what,' she said, gulping down the water and nearly choking in the process.

Zola put down her bag and turned to hide a burgeoning smile.

'Ma, you know Ma'Liphotho makes things up. Mbali just gave me a lift home. Didn't Thobile tell you that Okuhle asked me to help her with some work today?'

Nomsebenzi put her hands on her hips and turned sternly towards her eldest daughter.

'Zola, I don't care what you were doing. The gates at my house are locked at seven.' She walked past Zola without another word and slammed her bedroom door.

Covering her mouth to stifle her laughter, Zola crept into her bedroom and threw herself back on her bed. It gave a small bounce.

'So?' Thobile giggled, peeking out from under her blankets.

'So what?' Zola asked changing into her pyjamas.

'So Günter doesn't answer your calls and then suddenly you're outside in some fancy car with Mbali Thabethe doing "God-knows-what"? Tell me!' Thobile demanded.

'He just gave me a lift.' To her younger sister, the laughter in Zola's voice suggested there could be more to it. 'Now, sleep'.

Still laughing to herself, Zola lay back in bed taking it all in: the nosy neighbour and her mother's tantrum about the gate. It was too much not to share. She pulled her phone from her pocket and found a text from Mbali:

Your mom looked pissed!

Zola giggled. The text had set off a swarm of butterflies in her tummy. She typed:

Now I have some gossip for you ... well about you from my neighbour.

Zola felt like her lungs had somehow expanded – no matter how deeply she breathed, it wasn't enough to keep her from feeling like her head was spinning. Talking to Mbali had felt good and she wanted to keep feeling this way.

She lay in bed anxiously checking her phone for a reply. Nothing came, and Zola drifted off to sleep with her phone in her hand.

When she woke up in the morning to the sound of her mother's vengeful clattering of pots and pans in the kitchen, there was still no reply from Mbali, just two blue ticks next to her message.

Read. No response.

Zola groaned and stretched out under the covers, ignoring her mother's passive-aggressive insistence to no one in particular that they needed to get up and go to church.

Thobile jumped out of bed and immediately started complaining about having schoolwork to do, a test on Monday and countless other things; she couldn't go to church. That left Zola. Since Zola had come home from Germany, her mother had been trying to adjust and had for the most part left her to do her own thing. But after the drama about locking the gate from the previous night, Zola knew the honeymoon period was over.

'Good morning!' Zola said walking past her mother and her sister and heading for the bathroom, where she brushed her teeth staring at herself in the mirror. 'Firm, but respectful; firm but respectful ...' she rehearsed before coming back to face her mother.

'Zola? I thought you were bathing. We're going to be late for church and you know how much I hate that,' Nomsebenzi said, putting a pot of marinated chicken into the fridge.

'Ma, I've had a rough week. I'm going to stay home today and rest up for work tomorrow,' Zola said, swiftly moving back to her room so she didn't have to see Nomsebenzi's disappointment. Her phone flashed and she quickly grabbed it: it was just low battery. No calls, no texts. No word from Mbali.

She threw herself back onto the bed and scrolled through her phone. She quickly checked social media, flicking through the pictures of her friends back in Germany until she saw a page suggestion for Okuhle Msimanga.

Interesting, Zola thought. This was for a personal page, not the carefully curated business pages she had seen before. Clicking through, Zola found that the page was not private and had some recent snaps of Okuhle in the recovery clinic.

Zola scrolled through the pictures and stopped. There was Mbali. It was just the side of his face, but she recognised him immediately – it was taken with him in his car with a worried look on his face.

Okuhle had captioned it: 'My baby, so worried about me.'

Not her 'oldest friend', not someone who was 'like a brother' to her, but 'baby'. *Her* baby. The same baby who had driven Zola all the way home and sat outside her house laughing about nothing. So Mbali was

Okuhle's baby?

Zola was angry and confused. Sure, he'd sent her flowers, brought her lunch to work and seemed to be making some kind of mild advances, but was she reading too much into it? Maybe he was just being friendly …

But also, why would he lie about being Okuhle's boyfriend?

'And now, sis?' Thobile burst into the room.

'What do you want?' Zola replied grouchily.

Zola had never particularly liked sharing a room with her sister, but times like this made her hate it all the more.

'You've had Mom shaking since last night. What's going on with you?'

Zola sighed. 'I need my own place,' she announced.

Thobile rolled her eyes and started unpacking the laundry basket.

'Just one night living large and you're too good for this place,' she mumbled.

Seeing her normally perky sister looking so dejected, Zola suddenly felt guilty. She knew better than anyone how hard her mother had worked to make sure they had a good home. It wasn't a particularly nice home, but it was a *good* home. They'd never had to wonder if they'd have something to eat, they'd always had what they needed for school and they'd never struggled with anything.

'Sorry, Thobi. I'm just a little stressed out. Work stuff,' Zola said.

It was meant as an excuse but now that she thought about it, she really was stressed about work, seeing Okuhle in hospital, and now knowing her lunch and conversations with Mbali were completely out of line. Whether or not she'd known it at the time, she had violated the Girl Code.

When Zola's phone finally rang, she was in no hurry to answer it. Thobile tossed it towards her, glancing at the screen. 'It's Günter.'

Zola briefly considered ignoring the call, but thought better of it.

'Hey, Günter.' She smiled.

'Hey. I waited for your call last night. Did you forget about me?'

'No, no, sorry. I just got home kind of late,' Zola said. 'I thought you might be busy or out.'

'Oh. Okay.'

There was an ominous silence.

'About what your friend said, about helping me move to SA?' Günter said. Zola noticed he was speaking slower than usual – something was up. 'I spoke to my mom about it, and I don't think it's a good idea.'

Chapter 18

Mama's boys

Zola was quiet as Günter's words settled.

'Zola?' Günter pressed. 'Are you still there?'

'Yip,' Zola said sitting up in bed.

'Think about it – it really wouldn't work. I mean, I want to be with you and everything, but it works out better if we try to get you back home instead.'

There it was: 'home'. For ten years Zola had allowed herself to think of Germany as home, but she knew deeply that she already was home. South Africa wasn't Günter's home, but it was hers. Her conversation with Thobile just minutes ago had made her realise just how much she had taken for granted.

'You know what? This is my home, Günter,' Zola said calmly. 'I can't be in Germany without special permission. And … I can never find anyone to do my hair there and none of the foods I grew up with are in your stores …'

She wasn't arguing – it was just dawning on her that even though she'd enjoyed her life in Europe, she wasn't as desperate as she had been to find her way back there.

'Come on, Zola – things were better for both of us when you lived here. You said it yourself. Life in South Africa is hard. The crime alone has my mother worried – we see the stuff on the news and online all the time.'

And there it was, Günter's well-hidden Eurocentric views revealed courtesy of his beloved mother.

'This has nothing to do with your mother,' Zola said bitterly.

Günter's mother had always got to her. Her kindly ways had made Zola feel like an exotic pet Günter had brought home. There was something condescending about every nice thing she ever said or did for Zola.

'What do you mean it's got nothing to do with my mother?' Günter was clearly offended.

'I mean you're a grown man, Günter – you can make your own decisions. If you're too terrified to come to South Africa, the country I grew up in and have safely lived in for most of my life, just say so.'

'Have you stopped trying to get your Schengen residency visa?'

Mbali's probing flashed back to Zola. She remembered how Mbali had asked if Günter would survive South Africa, a criticism presented as a question. At the time it had irritated Zola that Mbali would have such opinions on Günter, but as it turned out, Mbali had been right.

'Why does it feel like I'm the only one trying to do anything for us to be together?' Zola asked.

Everything she was saying suddenly felt like a new realisation. She'd fought so hard to stay with Günter. Why wouldn't he even consider coming to be with *her*?

'Zola, it's different there ...'

Zola could hear that he was thinking about all the ways it was different – things he both did and didn't know anything about.

'You've lived here,' Günter continued. 'You saw for yourself – things just work better here. I don't know if I'd even be able to find a job in South Africa.' There was no regret in his voice – he sounded like everything was a foregone conclusion.

'And I couldn't find a job in Germany,' Zola said firmly. 'I *tried* to stay there, and it didn't work out for me.'

'Maybe we should pick this up later. You're being unreasonable. I can't talk to you when you're like this.'

'Actually, Günter, I'm always unreasonable.'

Zola hung up.

She lay down and stared at the ceiling, her vision blurring until the tears fell in thin rivulets and pooled in the creases of her ears.

Thobile crawled onto Zola's bed and hugged her.

'I'm glad you've decided to stay,' she said softly, holding Zola tighter.

Had she decided to stay? Zola didn't even know herself. But she was happy to be cuddling her sister. It rarely happened – hugs and kisses weren't really a thing in this household. Their mother usually just patted their backs on special occasions, and she never kissed them now that they were older.

'I'm so proud of you,' Thobile said. 'You stood your ground, you actually chose us.' She sounded surprised.

That was another thing Zola hadn't thought of that way. She hadn't considered that the choice between living in South Africa and going back to Germany was a choice between Günter and her family.

Zola and Thobile lay together for a while, the sound of the washing machine rumbling in the background as both of them quietly absorbed the moment. Then the washing machine beeped and Thobile got up to hang up her laundry outside.

Zola dragged herself out of bed and went into the bathroom. She wanted to wash the conversation with Günter off her body.

And this time she didn't have any hesitations – they really were through.

She ran a bath and sat in it, scrubbing her body as she thought about everything she had forgone to stay close to Günter – all the things she'd missed about her real home, all the things she hadn't done, just so Günter could stay close to his mother.

Like, Thobile had been just a kid when she'd left – and look at her now! A sensitive, capable, clever young woman. Zola hadn't even realised how much she'd missed the fact that she had a sister who seemed to intuitively know how she was feeling, who comforted her when she was low ...

'Zola!' Thobile shouted running into the house.

'What? What?' Panicked, Zola jumped out of the bathtub, still covered in soap, and stumbled out of the bathroom.

'That Mbali is here,' Thobile hissed.

'Here?' Zola hurried back into the bathroom.

Thobile laughed. 'He's outside in his car. You better hurry up before Ma'Liphotho sees him!'

Zola quickly rinsed off, trying to figure out what Mbali wanted and what she should wear. The lotion wouldn't rub into her skin fast enough, her jeans took forever to pull over her hips and her feet slid around in her sandals but eventually she was fully dressed and asking herself why 'Okuhle's baby' was at her gate, unannounced, first thing on a Sunday morning.

She squirted some perfume onto her neck and tried to look casual as she walked out of the house. Mbali was leaning against his car as if he belonged there just beyond the chicken-wire fence.

'Hi, Zola,' he said, pulling her into a hug.

Zola resisted, holding her arms at her sides.

'Is your mom home?' he asked.

Zola couldn't help laughing at the thought of Nomsebenzi, arms crossed in her pink gown, shouting at her grown daughter from the fence.

'No, she's at church. It'll be a few hours before she's back,' Zola said.

'Okay, phew. So, you want to go somewhere?'

As if it was a done deal, Mbali took her hand, led her to the passenger side of his car and opened her door.

Zola slid in, conscious of getting Mbali out of Ma'Liphotho's view as quickly as possible.

'Where are we going?' she asked as the car roared to life.

'Where do you want to go?'

Zola thought for a moment, then directed Mbali to the mall, making sure to avoid the worst roads.

'So, is there a reason why you've … kidnapped me from my house?'

Mbali smiled. 'You said you had some juicy gossip. I couldn't wait to hear it.'

It was almost sweet, but in the back of Zola's mind was the fact that she was driving around in her boss's boyfriend's car.

'Come on, Zola. Now that I'm here, you don't have anything to say?'

First Günter and now Mbali – the men in her life seemed determined to irritate her today. Her mood would not allow her to relax, laugh and joke with someone who had lied straight to her face.

'Oh, it was just about my mother's nosy neighbour. It was funny at the time …' Zola tried to bide her time before she could ask Mbali what she really wanted to ask him: if he was genuinely dating Okuhle.

'Tell me anyway,' Mbali pushed.

'Look … Why are you here?' Zola asked turning to Mbali. Sitting so close to him, she watched his face for signs, but at that moment his phone rang.

'It's my mom,' he said, at the same time as the car Bluetooth announced 'Ongama Thabethe, Mom'. 'She freaks out when I don't answer her calls. Let me just get this.'

Zola sighed and stared quietly ahead to give Mbali as much privacy as a moving two-seater car would allow.

'Mama, I'm on the road,' Mbali announced as a greeting.

'Cars have a hands-free option now, Mbali,' his mother snapped back, and Zola covered her mouth in shock at the snippy response.

'Yes, but I've got someone with me in the car—'

'Mbali!' Ongama interrupted sternly. 'I don't care who you have in the car with you. I am in Bali and I have taken time out of my holiday specifically to talk to you. The least you could do is greet me properly.'

Mbali sighed and looked to Zola, rolling his eyes. If he was looking for camaraderie, he got none because Zola was quite enjoying hearing Mbali being disciplined.

'Okay, I'll start again. Hi, Mama. How are you?' Mbali started afresh.

'I'm a lot better now that you're back together with Okuhle. Are you on your way to go see her now?'

Mbali grabbed to take the phone off its cradle, but then seemed to think better of it. He looked defeated.

'No, Ma. Where did you hear that?'

'From Priscilla. And I'm glad she won't be on my case about it any more. I'm done with the constant phone calls about how badly you are treating her daughter – it was getting embarrassing. And you know how much your father loves Okuhle,' she continued. 'He's thrilled too. You should call him.'

Mbali sighed heavily and avoided Zola's eyes even though he could feel her glaring at him.

'Can we talk about this later, Ma?' Mbali pleaded.

'I have things to do later. So, no. It was lucky that you were at Okuhle's house when she fell. Otherwise you know her mother would have found a way to blame you. Priscilla is a nut job,' Ongama continued.

Zola didn't bother to hide the fact that she was now listening intently. As if watching a tennis match, she looked from the phone while Mbali's mother was speaking to Mbali for his return volley.

'I really wish you and your friends would stay out of it,' Mbali said.

His mother had instantly sapped him of his carefree energy – right now he looked like he had the weight of the world on his shoulders.

'Stay out of it?' Ongama's irritation was clear even through the car speakers. 'I am your mother. Your actions will always be my business.

Now what you need to do is pull up your socks and start planning to marry that girl. I'm sick and tired of discussing this with Priscilla. It's getting embarrassing, and your father agrees.'

Mbali's response was to rub his eyes. He looked like a five year old needing a nap.

'Okay, Mama, we'll talk again soon,' he said as he drove into the mall's parking lot.

'Okay, my baby boy. I love you,' Ongama's voice softened and she cut the call.

When Mbali glanced at her, Zola glared back.

'Should I ask again?' Zola said, gripping the door handle as if ready to leap from the car at the slightest hint of a lie. 'What are you doing here? Why am I in your car? Why did you send me flowers when you not only have a girlfriend, but that girlfriend is my new boss?' Zola asked, her voice rising.

Mbali pulled into an open parking bay, turned off the car and sat back, closing his eyes while he composed himself.

'The truth. The truth is that ever since I saw you at that coffee shop for the interview, even though it was just once and just for a few seconds, I haven't been able to stop thinking about you.' Mbali's eyes pleaded with Zola to hear him out, and for once she sensed a vulnerability in him different to that of the little boy she had glimpsed when he was speaking to his mother.

But vulnerable or not, he was still a liar, and he had lied to her face. Nobody played fast and loose with Zola like that.

She scrunched her nose with disgust and clicked her tongue, stretching out the sound as long as she possibly could.

'You disgust me.'

She climbed out of his car and walked away into the mall.

Chapter 19

Advice from an unlikely source

Zola walked through the mall grateful that Mbali at least had the grace not to chase after her.

The nerve of him! she thought, marching angrily past clothing shops she would normally have stopped to look at. It had been bad enough seeing Okuhle's 'baby' post, but having their relationship confirmed by Mbali's own mother and then having him try to woo her just seconds later … It made her feel dirty.

Zola sat down on a bench and realised that she didn't even have her wallet. Now she was stranded. She scrolled through her phone trying to think of someone who could help her out. She landed on her cousin Zozo's details and cringed at the thought, but she had no choice. She pressed dial and an annoying caller tune blasted into her ear.

'Hey, cuzzy!' Zozo screamed into the phone.

'Hey, Zozo. Listen, where are you?' Zola tried to sound friendly rather than desperate.

'I'm with Thabo. You know, Sundays are for lovers,' Zozo said laughing.

'I'm really sorry to interrupt, but I need your help.' Zola sighed. She had never imagined needing Zozo's help, but here she was.

'Anything, cuzzy. What's up?' Zozo was all ears and actually sounded excited.

'I'm stranded at the mall in Spruitview, and I don't have my wallet. Can you come fetch me?'

'Let me talk to Thabo quickly …' Zozo didn't bother with the hold button, and Zola heard her baby voice giggling and cooing before she got back on the line. 'Okay, wait by the gate – we'll be there in a few minutes! See ya!'

Relieved, Zola found her way to the exit and walked slowly across the open car park to the gate, the sun blazing down and searing the back of her neck.

On the street, chattering women in church uniforms walked past, little kids sucked on ice packets unbothered by the heat and men in cars zoomed past, some hooting, some shouting suggestively at her from their open windows.

She was miserable, and it was all Mbali's fault.

Finally, a rickety taxi pulled up with Zozo hanging out of the window shouting her name.

'Zola! Hurry up!'

Zola climbed into the taxi, and perched on the edge of a seat she was sure would tip over at the slightest provocation, greeting Thabo and his friend in the front.

'Women are a problem, seriously,' Thabo said to no one in particular. 'How did you get to the mall without your wallet? How did you think you were going to get home?' He glared at Zola through the rear-view mirror.

'Thabo, don't talk to my cousin like that,' Zozo sprang to Zola's defence. 'She's been living in Germany and things work differently there.

She probably got confused.'

Offensive, but she meant well. Zola studying in Germany was a point of pride for everyone in her family, even Zozo – and now a random taxi driver she had never even seen before knew about it.

'Yeah, but still,' Thabo mumbled. 'She needs to know she's back here now – it's not like she's new to the township. Next time, sisi, you'll walk home.'

It took all of Zola's self-control to keep her mouth shut and be grateful for the free ride.

'If you don't leave her alone, Thabo, I swear we'll get out of this rickety old taxi right now!' Zozo shouted, standing up and then hastily sitting down again as they lurched over a pothole.

Thabo's friend turned around to look at Zola.

'What does my taxi have to do with her now?' he asked, his voice rough and hoarse as gravel.

'Easy, easy,' Thabo said tapping his friend on the shoulder.

Zola sat quietly biting the inside of her cheek. They weren't on the route to her house – in fact, they'd driven straight past the road to her side of the township and were heading further and further away.

'Where are we going?' Zola whispered to Zozo.

'Carwash,' Zozo said as if that had been the plan all along. Then she smiled. 'So, I heard you have a new boyfriend. An older guy who drives some fancy sports car.' She raised her hand in a high-five.

Zola pulled Zozo's hand down. 'Who did you hear that from?'

'We *all* heard,' Thabo chimed in. 'You might as well have been on TV. Ma'Liphotho can't stop talking about how disrespectful you've become since you came home.'

'Oh, this is *that* Zola?' Thabo's friend laughed gratingly. It sounded painful, like a dry cough. 'The nasty girl who does all kinds of things in cars?'

Zola felt her heat rise. Even though this wasn't true, the neighbours were talking – just like her mother had predicted. Another reason to curse the day she had ever met Mbali.

'But if you have a sugar daddy, why are *we* the ones who have to come pick you up from the mall?' Thabo's friend asked.

Zola was annoyed, but she was in their car and she was now even further away from home than she'd been before. She'd have to be careful with these guys.

'I don't have a sugar daddy. Ma'Liphotho is making things up as usual. I just got a lift from work,' Zola explained.

'You'll tell me the real story when it's just the two of us,' Zozo whispered, nudging her cousin.

Zola nodded, just to get Zozo off her back. She had enough to worry about without this unnecessary drama.

They were welcomed to the carwash by the smell of braai meat and the sound of speakers vibrating and blasting amapiano, which set Zozo off. She was already dancing and whistling the tune of the song before she'd jumped out of the car. She held out her hands inviting Zola to dance, but Zola just shook her head.

'They don't dance like that in Germany,' Thabo laughed, taking Zozo's hand and leading her further into the carwash.

Zola followed, trying to act cool, like one of the regulars. Like she came to places like this all the time, even though her mother had never allowed it when she was young, and by the time she was old enough, she'd already been in Germany. And no, they didn't dance like Zozo in Germany.

Zola followed Zozo's lead and sat down on a crate, taking a cider from an ice bucket Thabo had set in front of them before disappearing into a group of friends.

'You know, Zola, I really miss you,' Zozo started, taking a sip from her bottle. 'We used to be so close. Do you remember?'

Zola smiled. 'I do. We just grew apart. It happens.'

Zozo pouted her lips and gave Zola an accusing look. 'We didn't grow apart. We've always been different – you just started thinking your different was better than mine,' she said sadly.

Zola took a deep breath. Today seemed to be a day for home truths – starting with Günter, everyone she'd spoken to seemed to have had an axe to grind with her. Still, she was rather surprised by her cousin's sincerity.

'I'm really sorry, Zozo,' Zola said.

'I just worry about you, you know?' Zozo smiled sadly. 'And I want you to know that I'm here for you. I might not understand everything you say, but I can listen.' Zozo put her hand on her cousin's.

Zola nodded, feeling a prickle of tears. She was starting to feel overwhelmed – and she knew that if she spoke just then, she'd probably burst into tears in front of all these people.

Zozo squeezed her hand and they continued to drink in silence until Zola realised she should call her mother – Nomsebenzi would be back from church by now. She wouldn't be happy about where Zola was, but the fact that she was out with Zozo would make it better. Less like things were spinning out of control.

She pulled out her phone and noticed there was a message from Mbali:

Can I see you? Just hear me out this one time. I promise, if you never want to see me again after that, you never have to.

Zola groaned. The drama never seemed to end – it was one thing after the next.

'Cuz, you know the guy everyone seems to think is my sugar daddy?' Zola started.

Zozo nodded attentively and moved closer to hear her over the loud music.

'Well, he isn't really a sugar daddy. We met, kind of, when I went for a job interview. It didn't work out with his company and I got a job somewhere else,' Zola explained.

Zozo looked at her intently, her drink just inches from her lips but frozen as she listened. She seemed to be taking her new role as confidant very seriously.

'When I got my job, he sent me flowers to the office. I didn't understand it then, but it really upset my boss,' Zola said skimming over the details. 'Then the next day he brought another bouquet, and delivered them himself. He brought lunch and we ate it outside. Then my boss arrived and saw him, and there was a really weird vibe,' Zola continued, with Zozo nodding constantly through the one-sided conversation. 'It turns out they know each other – I saw them together yesterday and then I found out they've actually been dating for a really long time. Like, since they were teenagers.'

Zozo's eyes widened. 'He's your boss's *boyfriend*? And she *saw* you together?'

'Yip. I was going to ask him about it today when we went to the mall, but then his mother called and I didn't really need to because she was talking marriage ...' Zola explained.

'But your boss, when she saw you, she didn't *say* anything? No tantrum, no fight? And you still have your job?'

'Yes,' Zola said. 'She told me they were old friends, that they'd grown up together. She did kind of warn me off him at first, but she didn't act like his girlfriend – not even when I saw them together.'

Zozo sipped her drink, thoughtfully processing Zola's drama and weighing things up.

'I don't think she really is his girlfriend,' she said finally. 'There has to be some misunderstanding. What did he say about it?'

Zola looked down at her phone. 'To be honest, I didn't want to hear anything more from him. I mean, what kind of person does this kind of thing? And it's not like we were even dating,' Zola consoled herself.

'But you like him.'

'Not really,' Zola said quickly. 'It's just ... you know ... I don't want all this drama to affect my work.'

Zozo chuckled to herself. 'You wouldn't be this angry if you didn't like him at least a bit. I think you should hear him out. Get his side of the story before you decide to cut him off.'

Zola was surprised by how level-headed Zozo was. It appeared she'd underestimated her. And what was the harm in giving Mbali one more chance to explain himself? Zola couldn't exactly get more confused than she felt right now. But there was only one way she could guarantee she was getting the true story.

She picked up her phone and sent Mbali a text message:

I'll hear you out, but on one condition. Okuhle has to be there.

With that out of the way, Zola sent a text to her mother and put her phone back in her pocket. She couldn't help but hope she had misunderstood the whole situation between Okuhle and Mbali.

So maybe she did like him.

Chapter 20

Being reasonable

Mbali sat at his desk trying to figure out how he could set up a meeting with both Zola and Okuhle. It was a messy situation and he had no one to blame but himself.

Of all the women he could find himself so irrepressibly attracted to, why did it have to be Zola? The more he spoke to her, the more reasons he found to want to spend even more time with her. Okuhle just wouldn't understand.

The day Okuhle had fallen down the stairs had forced him to realise that it really wasn't all her fault. He'd definitely had a hand in making her believe things would eventually work out between them – even though he now knew with certainty that he'd really had no intention of working things out with her.

Mbali still clearly remembered how things had ended between them, although he knew Okuhle had a version that was probably very different.

They had both just graduated. Their relationship had survived high school and the wild university years. Mbali would visit Okuhle in Cape Town, and she would come to Johannesburg to see him whenever she could. They'd spoken on the phone for hours every day. But when they had finally organised their lives to be in the same city, they just hadn't clicked.

But only Mbali had seemed to feel it.

Okuhle had wanted to get married right away. She'd had plans to continue studying, but she'd also wanted commitment. Mbali had been consumed by plans to build his empire, and had worked tirelessly on that right from the start. Looking back, he could see that he'd been at his most ambitious then. Settling down had been the furthest thing from his mind.

'It's not a suicide pact, babe,' Okuhle had said when Mbali first said he wasn't ready. And perhaps he'd hidden behind his ambitions, because he hadn't been able to confess that his feelings for Okuhle had felt increasingly platonic.

Even their friends from high school had piled on the pressure – and he'd bowed to it, never quite committing to buying a ring, but too scared to actually break things off with her. He'd effectively maintained the relationship out of fear of hurting Okuhle, because even though he wasn't ever in love with her, he did care about her.

But eventually he'd been unable to keep up the façade.

'I don't want to hold you back from your dream while I chase mine,' Mbali remembered saying.

He also remembered the look on Okuhle's face. Her eyes had filled with tears and her mouth had dropped open as if she'd been punched in the gut.

'Why are you doing this to me?' she'd asked in disbelief. He hadn't been able to answer her then, and he doubted he'd be able to answer the same question now.

So he'd lied.

'We're meant to be, Hlehle. I know it, I can feel it, and I know in the end it will always be you and me. Just not right now. I have nothing to offer you now.'

He'd spent the rest of that night fielding calls from his parents, her parents and a distraught Okuhle after she'd gone back to her parents' home for the night.

Now he was going to have to do that all over again, except this time he was going to have to tell her the truth: there was no future for Mbali and Okuhle.

'Fuck,' he whispered to himself.

He'd never imagined he would be in this position again – but things had gone too far. When he'd broken up with Okuhle, he'd expected her to move on, find someone who would love her and make her so happy she'd forget all about her childhood sweetheart. He'd really hoped that would give him the space to move on too. She was beautiful, successful and smart – there was really no reason for her to be alone and desperate.

And yet she was.

And this wasn't the first time she had sabotaged his relationship. She'd introduced herself to one woman as his long-suffering wife. She'd turned up to an event he'd attended and confronted his date, publicly claiming he was cheating on her. That time their parents had become involved, fuelling her belief that in the end he'd grow up and become the perfect husband she was waiting for.

Mbali sighed and checked his phone.

It was a little after midnight – in Tokyo it was very early in the morning but the office would be open. His father would be setting up for his meetings or crunching numbers with his banker.

It was time to make the call.

Half the world away, Elias Thabethe was doing just that.

He was a stern man who liked everything to be done to his exacting standards. Mbali, his only son, always fell short of his expectations.

Since Mbali was a child, they had argued and fought over just about everything.

Mbali resented Elias but he was desperate – right now, Elias was the only person Mbali trusted to advise him.

'Boy!' his father answered the phone.

'Baba,' Mbali greeted. 'How are you?'

His father grunted his response – his usual answer. Elias wasn't one for pleasantries, and was not an easy man to get along with. He liked to get straight to the point.

Mbali often wondered how his father had managed all his infidelities when he was so difficult to like. Mbali usually ended their conversations thinking his mother was a saint.

'I'm surprised you're awake,' Elias said. 'I know how much you like your sleep.'

Mbali bit his tongue, and decided to ignore his father's insinuation that he was lazy.

'We do things differently, Dad,' Mbali simply said.

'There's a wrong and a right way of doing things,' Elias boomed. 'Maybe if I hadn't handed you everything on a silver platter you'd understand.'

Elias could go on like this for hours, taking apart Mbali's every habit and blaming his every failure on him being spoilt –like he wasn't top of his class because he'd never walked barefoot to school. Even though Mbali had practically been raised by his grandmother, his father had watched his every move from afar. From the other side of the world, Elias had been informed if Mbali had misbehaved at school, or passed or failed a test. He'd spoken to him mostly to admonish him.

But as much as Mbali dreaded speaking to his father, Elias was also the only person he trusted to advise him because he cut straight to the chase. In a certain sense, it was his gift. Possibly his only one.

'Mom asked me to call you.' Mbali couldn't shake the habit of using his mother as a shield, the buffer between them.

'Ah, yes.' Elias made a sound that stood for mirth, but the pride in his voice was also unmistakable. 'I've heard your news and I must say I've been waiting for you to finally do the right thing.'

So the 'news' had travelled. Mbali's parents had been misinformed, likely by Okuhle herself. She'd probably read too much into him helping her when she was hurt, and his humane gesture had somehow been translated into a marriage proposal.

Mbali tensed. He knew his conversation with his father could go one of two ways – and it was clear that this was going to go badly.

'Dad, there is no news. I tried to explain that to Mom earlier,' Mbali said irritably. 'I don't know where you've all got this from.'

'Real men don't whine,' Elias admonished. 'Talk like a man – not like a little girl. What are you saying, Mbali?'

Mbali took a deep breath to settle his own anger. 'I'm saying there is no news. Things between Okuhle and I are the same as they always were. We're not even together.'

Elias was quiet for a while, probably trying to figure out where he had gone wrong; why his son always seemed to do the opposite of what Elias wanted.

'When are you going to grow up, Mbali? Okuhle is the one, I know this for sure. Girls like that don't come around every day. If you don't get your act together soon, a smarter man will beat you to it.'

Mbali lost his patience. 'That's *exactly* the point, Baba. I *wish* someone would snatch Okuhle up and finally put an end to this madness. Okuhle is my childhood friend. I don't want anything more from her. I don't see her in any other way and I never will. I just want everyone to understand that and let us both move on.'

'Hmm,' Elias said thoughtfully. 'You're a bigger idiot than I thought.'

Mbali leant back in his chair and massaged his neck. 'Dad, please can you help me? I just need everyone, especially Okuhle, to understand that we're done. There isn't going to be a wedding. How do I tell her that?'

Elias sighed. On the other end of the phone, Mbali could hear a pen being tapped on a desk. Beyond the huge glass windows, he knew, the early-morning sun would be glinting across the Tokyo skyline.

'The only thing I can help you with is advice,' Elias said gruffly. 'I can't do this for you, understand? You need to speak to Okuhle first. She's the one driving this whole thing. But be aware that once you break things off with her, there won't be any turning back.'

Mbali was already preparing for the worst.

Chapter 21

In recovery

Monday morning and Okuhle felt weak. She'd been up all night stressing about the expo – it was only two weeks away now, but with one working arm there wasn't much she could do. Even though she'd only been at the recovery centre for a weekend, she felt like things at work were already spiralling out of control. The thought of what might happen without her physically at the helm made her anxious.

She pressed the call button and summoned a nurse to help her pack and get ready to leave.

'Okuhle, you need to take things easy,' said the matronly nurse. 'I really don't think leaving is a good idea – you can't even pack your own bag. You'll be able to do far more at the office if you first let yourself recover.'

But Okuhle shook her head, grabbing what she could with her one working arm, and stubbornly pressing on with her plans to get to the office.

'I'll make it work,' she said. 'I can't do anything from here.'

With her bags ready and waiting, Okuhle tried to call Mbali one more time. She hadn't heard from him since he'd left the centre on Saturday evening with Zola, and that only added to her anxiety.

Her accident had been well timed, though – he'd spent the whole of Saturday looking after her. Clearly it had made Mbali see just how wrong he'd been for side-lining her. Even though she'd been in agony, she'd seen and appreciated the love and concern in his eyes when he'd got to her house and found her sprawled on the floor crying. And he hadn't missed a beat – he'd driven her to the hospital and stayed with her throughout the doctor's assessments. He'd even made the booking for her at the recovery centre, and when she'd thought he was about to abandon her there, he'd stayed, only popping out briefly to freshen up and bring her clothes and some of her favourite treats.

If that wasn't love, Okuhle didn't know what was. But now he was gone again. It made no sense. What had changed?

When her Uber arrived, Okuhle climbed in, settled herself and tried to call Mbali again. This time he answered.

'You checked out of the recovery centre,' he said skipping past the usual greetings.

Okuhle couldn't tell if he was tired, angry or both. It was clear that he wasn't pleased.

'I need to go to work,' Okuhle said stubbornly. 'You know I can't afford to mess up this expo – my mom will kill me.'

'Your mom,' Mbali breathed a sigh. 'Okuhle, I've been hearing some things. What exactly have you been telling her?'

Okuhle paused to think. She hadn't told her mother anything that wasn't true: she'd gushed about how well Mbali was taking care of her, how things finally looked like they were coming together. Nothing else.

'I just told her she didn't have to worry because you were taking care of me,' Okuhle said.

'Then why did she tell my mother we were back together?' Mbali asked angrily. 'And why are my parents both on my case about getting married?'

Okuhle flinched – even though it was her dearest wish, she recognised that Mbali's buttons had been pushed. The last thing she wanted was to scare him off. Even though she'd told her mother how good she'd felt about Mbali, how everything had felt so right between them, she hadn't specifically said they were back together.

'Mbali, I'm not crazy. I wouldn't make up something like that, and neither would my mom. I think it's a misunderstanding – a broken telephone. You know how excitable they all are. And they've been planning our wedding since we were infants. They were just saying what they've been hoping to hear.'

Mbali took a breath to steady himself. Maybe this was his moment to come clean. It wasn't ideal, it would be more decent to do it in person, but he wasn't sure how much longer he could wait. Especially as far as Zola was concerned – he really wanted to take that further. The whole Günter situation was enough of an obstacle – he didn't need an Okuhle situation as well. And now Zola had asked to meet him and Okuhle together ... It would really be best if Okuhle heard it like this first.

'Okuhle, you know I care about you,' Mbali's voice became gentle. 'And I'll always be there for you. I just ... I can't love you the way you want me to.'

Okuhle gasped. She hadn't been expecting Mbali to blow up at her about their parents' gossip, but this turn of events was absolutely unacceptable to her.

'*What?*' She didn't care that the Uber driver nearly jumped out of his seat at her sudden change of mood. 'Mbali, are you *incapable* of love? Do you have some kind of deficiency that makes it impossible to think about anyone but yourself? Because it definitely looks that way.'

The driver switched off the radio, but Okuhle didn't care who heard her. 'I haven't even made it home from hospital and you're tearing me down? What is *wrong* with you?'

Mbali had known Okuhle would fight back. Their normal pattern was that she would blame him for everything, and he would accept that blame if that's what it took to be understood. But the pain in her voice still made him feel guilty. He considered taking it all back, but he knew he had done that too many times and it had never made anything better – things had only got much, much worse.

'Am I ... unlovable?' she continued, now whimpering. 'Maybe there's something wrong with me ...'

'No, Hlehle, there's probably something wrong with me,' Mbali soothed as if speaking to a small child. 'And that shouldn't be your problem. You're a gorgeous, smart, successful woman. You deserve so much more than the half-baked life I would give you. I love you enough to know that.'

Through her self-pity, Okuhle saw red. Mbali wasn't thinking about her at all. As usual it was all about him, all about what he wanted. It didn't matter to him that all she wanted was him – any way she could have him.

'And what if I was happy with half-baked love? What if that was enough for me?' Okuhle tried not to cry. She'd already shed too many tears over Mbali and this was not the time to be weak – this was her chance to fight for the dream she had for the both of them.

'But *I* wouldn't be happy,' Mbali admitted. 'I know I've hurt you. I've done many things I shouldn't have, but I deserve to be happy too, and spending the rest of my life being not good enough, not loving you enough, not giving you enough of me – I couldn't stand it.'

Breathing heavily, Okuhle felt she was on the verge of a panic attack as Mbali continued his speech.

'You know better than anyone how much my parents' marriage has messed me up. I don't want to make the same mistakes. I don't want to be like my father, constantly hurting the woman I claim to love,' Mbali confessed. 'I'm sure you've heard about my mother's latest trip. I don't want you to have to take trips to Bali to recover from being married to me.'

Okuhle's mother had always said as much, and now Mbali was finally admitting his family's dysfunction. But for Okuhle it was already too late. Too late for him to try and protect her. She already needed the trip to Bali. She already needed to recover.

'Is that what you were thinking when you sent another woman my favourite flowers knowing full well I'd see them?' Okuhle asked. 'You knew that would hurt me, but you did it anyway. Of all the women in the world, it had to be Zola, my newest employee.'

Mbali sucked in a sharp breath. Okuhle's words stung. And yes, on some level he had known that what he was doing was wrong. But he hadn't been able to help himself. He'd already decided that he wanted Zola before Okuhle had even hired her. And, if he was honest with himself, Okuhle's feelings were nothing more than collateral damage.

'But, Okuhle, before it was Zola it was someone else. You would have been hurt either way. I didn't hurt you by sending Zola flowers – I hurt you by lying to you,' Mbali admitted. 'I thought I was doing the right thing, that eventually you would figure it out and move on, but I was wrong. You can hate me for that – I had it coming. I should never have promised you that we'd end up together. Even then I knew we wouldn't.'

For Okuhle, this was too much. All her words seemed to ball in her throat and all she could do was breathe into the phone. On his side of the line, Mbali held his phone to his ear, listening to her breathing and not saying a word.

They sat like that as the Uber drove through the city towards Okuhle's house, Okuhle sitting in the back seat feeling shattered. She wanted so badly to hate Mbali, to despise him, but all the love she'd packed away in her heart for all these years made that impossible.

'I'm home now, Mbali,' she said as the Uber parked outside her house.

'Do you need anything?' Mbali asked dutifully.

'I need a trip to Bali,' Okuhle said, finally hanging up.

Okuhle dragged her suitcase into her house, pain shooting through her arm and up her neck with every step. This was not the time to be weak.

She would have liked to have stayed at the recovery centre a while longer, but she had work to do. The African Wedding Expo wouldn't organise itself.

Chapter 22

Nothing but the truth

Zola's heart pounded in her chest. Every morning when she came to work she expected see Okuhle. Luckily for Zola, although Okuhle sent regular emails relating to the expo and to work in general, she hadn't been to the office all week. Zola was relieved – she didn't know how she would act around her after she'd asked to sit with her and Mbali to have that very uncomfortable conversation.

For her part, Okuhle's emails did seem different. To start with, she stuck to emailing only during working hours, and Zola had been able to leave the office on time every day. And there were neither friendly remarks nor jealous attacks – just clean, clear professionalism, which oddly enough felt cold compared to the Okuhle that Zola had first met.

That was fair, Zola decided. In fact, it was more than fair. Although Zola's work was meticulous, Okuhle could easily have found a reason to fire her – and Zola wouldn't even have blamed her if she had. The situation with Mbali was complicated, and in Okuhle's position Zola didn't think she would have managed such cool, calm discussions about vendors and plotting delivery routes. Not with the woman who had caught her boyfriend's eye.

'So, *I* heard you went to go see the boss lady in hospital when she got hurt,' Khanyisa teased one morning.

Zola flared her nostrils. Did Khanyisa also know about Mbali? Was that the office gossip?

'Who told you that?' Zola snapped, not hiding her irritation.

'Chill, Zola. What's your problem?' Khanyisa said defensively. 'I heard it from Thulare – he got an email signed from both of you last Saturday. Anyway, I just wanted to know how badly she was hurt. It's really not like her to stay away from the office for so long – especially not when we're working on such a big project.'

'Sorry,' Zola said. 'I have a lot on my mind. And yes, I did go to see her – she asked me to come in to help her write some emails. She has some broken bones, which makes it impossible for her to drive or type. I'm sure she'll be back as soon as she can.'

But Khanyisa was not one to be easily pacified. Shaking her head, she rolled her chair back to her desk and didn't speak to Zola for the rest of the day. In fact, no one spoke to Zola on most days. She kept to herself, only speaking to her colleagues when she needed to.

With everything else going on in her life, she hadn't gotten to know anyone in the office personally yet, and maybe it was for the best. It meant she could easily keep things to herself.

The week ended with no sign of Okuhle. Zola made her way home, taking one taxi after the another. But there was none of that Friday feeling – she was still anxious about the day she'd have to finally face Okuhle. Mbali had called Zola and she had rejected his calls, determined to keep to her word. She wouldn't talk to him and she wouldn't read his texts. She didn't want to hear from him until she could be sure that what he was saying was true.

'Zola, you haven't been yourself lately. Is everything okay? How's work going?' Nomsebenzi asked that evening, sitting herself down at the foot of Zola's bed.

Zola shrugged. 'I'm just tired, Ma. We have this huge wedding expo coming up on Friday next week and I just want to prove myself.' She deftly omitted the part she knew her mother wouldn't want to hear.

Nomsebenzi smiled with pride. 'Okay. I know you can do anything you put your mind to. My girl will always impress.' And then, as if trying to seem comfortable with the idea, Nomsebenzi asked Zola about Günter.

Of course she didn't approve of him. Even as grown-up as Zola was now, it was hard for Nomsebenzi to accept that she was dating anyone, let alone a foreign man she had never physically met. On the rare occasions they had spoken on the phone, she had hardly understood a word he'd said, his accented English too thick for her ear.

'I haven't heard you speaking to him in a long time. Is everything okay?' Nomsebenzi asked.

'No, actually,' Zola said shaking her head. 'We broke up.'

This was uncomfortable: Zola and her mother had never spoken about boys, and Zola had never actually introduced Günter to her mother as her boyfriend. When Nomsebenzi had first seen him in the background of a video call, Zola had told her mother he was just a visiting friend, and left her to piece the story together herself.

'Ey, I'm sorry to hear that.' Nomsebenzi didn't know what else to say on the matter.

'Long distance is hard, Mom,' Zola said. Even though she didn't show it, she had always craved a close relationship with her mom. She'd wanted to be able to tell her everything, but found that Nomsebenzi overreacted to just about everything.

'Does it have anything to do with the man in the car from the other day?' Nomsebenzi asked, smoothing Zola's bed.

THE THING WITH ZOLA

'You mean my "sugar daddy"?' Zola teased.

She watched her mother's eyes widen and knew she'd gone too far.

'I'm *joking*, Mama. He's not my sugar daddy, and he's not even that much older than me. And I wouldn't say he was the reason for my break-up, although he did have something to do with it,' Zola admitted. 'He helped me see certain things about Günter for myself.'

Nomsebenzi considered Zola for a short while as she tried to decide if she wanted to know more. 'Certain things like what?' she finally asked.

'Like that I was the only one making an effort. I wanted to go back to Germany and Günter wanted that too, but things didn't work out that way, right?' Zola said. 'But when I asked Günter if he would come to South Africa, he had all kinds of excuses. And he wasn't exactly original – his first objection was simply "crime". He wasn't willing to think about it or even to try.'

Nomsebenzi's chest swelled with pride over her daughter's decision.

'It's never a good idea to chase a man,' Nomsebenzi said. 'Your whole life can never revolve around somebody else, or you'll start acting crazy and doing things you don't understand. You should always love yourself more than you love anyone else,' she said gently. Then, in a rare gesture, Nomsebenzi took Zola's hand and kissed her palm.

Zola felt a warmth spread through her. Everything was going to be okay.

'Goodnight then, sisi. I'll try to be quiet in the morning when I leave. You need your rest,' Nomsebenzi said, walking out and turning off the lights.

For the first time in days, Zola drifted into a peaceful sleep.

Saturday morning and Zola woke up smiling. Her mother had kept her promise and left quietly for work. Thobile had followed suit and gone to her Saturday classes without making any noise, and even Mbali had stopped calling and texting.

Zola stretched. She would enjoy having the house to herself.

A short while later she was eating a big bowl of cereal in front of the TV in her pyjamas. It was the kind of weekend she'd been craving – no plans, no checking her phone, no drama.

But she had celebrated too soon: when her phone rang, the shrill sound immediately disturbed her newfound peace. Okuhle. Zola certainly didn't want to talk to Mbali's girlfriend, but she had to talk to the woman who signed her pay cheques.

'Hi, Okuhle. How are you feeling?'

Okuhle's voice was low and sombre. 'Honestly, Zola, I'm far from fine. And that's what I want to talk to you about.'

Zola felt herself go cold.

'It's got nothing to do with work, and I want you to understand that this conversation is between two women, not between an employer and employee,' Okuhle said in a slow practised monologue. 'We can't let this affect our work together, because honestly as far as work is concerned, you've been my life raft.' Okuhle's voice cracked, and Zola could tell she was only just holding it together.

Zola felt sorry for Okuhle – they were both in a difficult position. Both grateful for each other and yet at odds at the same time. Zola listened without speaking, giving Okuhle a chance to say what she needed to say.

'This is such a strange feeling.' Okuhle laughed through what were now open tears. 'I mean, I'm so glad I met you, but at the same time it's been a freakin' nightmare.' Okuhle laughed sadly again. 'Zola? You're really quiet.'

'I'm just listening,' Zola said. 'I'm trying to understand what all this is about.'

Even with Okuhle's assurance, it was hard for Zola to separate her working life from her personal life. If they hadn't worked together, none of this would even matter – Zola might not even have known Mbali already had a woman in his life.

THE THING WITH ZOLA

'I'm sure you already know that I want to talk about Mbali,' Okuhle said, blowing out her breath. 'I think my first mistake was misrepresenting myself and my intentions,' she admitted.

'Yes,' Zola agreed. 'If you'd been honest from the beginning, things would never have gotten to this point. If I'd known anything was going on between you and Mbali, I would have steered well clear of him, but you chose to manipulate me instead. I don't appreciate that.'

Surprised by Zola's candour, Okuhle took a sharp breath in. She didn't disagree. Even though when she'd tried to steer Zola away from Mbali, in her mind she'd been protecting a possible friendship with her new employee. Clearly she hadn't gone about it the right way.

'I get that, and I'm sorry. I shouldn't have burdened you with my hurt. To be honest, I panicked,' Okuhle said.

'Hmm,' Zola hummed, waiting for Okuhle to get to the point. 'Okuhle, sorry, but you're beating about the bush. You've showered me with platitudes but I still don't understand why we're even in this position in the first place.'

Okuhle was taken aback – she hadn't seen this feisty side of Zola, and she was beginning to understand what Mbali saw in her. Zola could stand up to him, challenge him in a way Okuhle knew she never would. Never thought she could.

'I'll start at the beginning ...' Okuhle said nervously, and the more Okuhle explained, the worse Zola felt for her. She was glad Mbali wasn't there – she would have hated witnessing Okuhle having to face him after everything they had put each other through. And Zola was relieved she didn't have to physically face Okuhle either. Even after hearing Mbali's mother talk about Okuhle, the reality was much more than Zola anticipated. Mbali had been Okuhle's first love – it was only natural that she'd had expectations.

'... so it turns out Mbali only called it a break to spare my feelings,' Okuhle continued. 'He'd fallen out of love with me, but he was too much of a coward to tell it to me straight. I thought we'd end up together and every time I thought someone threatened that, I lashed out. With you, it was different. I know Mbali. I know how he woos a woman and when I saw him try it with you, right under my nose, I needed to put an end to it,' she said.

Zola could piece together the rest of the story herself. Mbali had made a move on her and Okuhle caught on before she had, and tried to nip it in the bud.

'Okuhle, if I had known that, I would never even have entertained the idea of him,' Zola said truthfully. 'I would have told him myself that what he was doing was wrong, and I wouldn't have any part of it. I'm so sorry I was part of something that hurt you so much.'

On opposite sides of the phone, the two women sighed simultaneously. The conversation was heavy and Zola was starting to sweat. But at least everything was out in the open now.

'I think you should know that Mbali has never said a bad word about you,' Zola said. 'Every time he has spoken about you, it has been with love. Even though things haven't worked out between the two of you, I know he cares about you.'

'But it isn't enough, is it?' Okuhle said. 'Because even after everything, I still love Mbali.'

'So what now?' Zola asked.

'If you still want to get to know Mbali, I don't blame you. He's a great guy. I won't hold it against you and I won't stand in your way.'

Chapter 23

A clean slate

Zola sat on the couch staring at the TV but not watching it. The only thing on her mind was Okuhle's words.

She didn't understand Mbali at all. He might be a 'great guy', but how could he have been so cruel to Okuhle? And then also so kind? It was obvious he cared for her – it was in the way he spoke about her and the things he did – but in his attempts to protect her from heartbreak he had completely devastated her.

By the end of their conversation Zola had hardly recognised Okuhle's voice. Okuhle had cried and heaved and worked so hard to stop herself from sobbing that her confident voice had become nothing but a hoarse whisper.

And Zola couldn't shake a feeling about Mbali that she couldn't really name, a curiosity about who he was. Despite herself, she'd found herself wondering what it would feel like to be held by him, what his hands would feel like on *her* body. What thoughts passed through his mind when he saw her. What his kiss would taste like.

These feelings came to her in a rush, as if her suspicions about him and Okuhle had blocked them all along.

This was not the romance she had wanted for herself – in fact, right now she wanted no romance of any kind – but every now and then in the past week she'd found herself thinking of Mbali, of the way he laughed, of the smell of his cologne … of just *him*. She didn't know anybody like him; still, she had never been so conflicted. There was no way she could trust herself to keep a level head when she spoke to him. Not yet.

Zola sat with her feelings, soaking in them trying to understand them, but she was stumped. She needed a sounding board and the first person she thought of was Zozo. She would never have thought of telling her ditzy cousin anything until recently, but like everyone in her life of late, it seemed she had misjudged her.

Hey cuz, what are you doing? Zola typed.

If Zozo was with Thabo, she knew it would be hours before she replied, but to her surprise, Zozo replied instantly.

Thabo broke up with me.

Zola gasped. She had never liked Thabo, but she knew Zozo adored him and she really had thought he'd loved Zozo too.

Ah, I'm so sorry, cuz. Do you want to grab some lunch and talk about it? Zola offered.

Again Zozo replied quickly.

On my way.

Zola got dressed in a hurry, pulling on a long flowy dress that always made her feel beautiful, and some strappy sandals.

When Zozo arrived she was as devastated as Zola had imagined. Weeping hysterically, the younger woman walked through the gate, and coughed and spluttered as she dragged herself across the front yard and through the door.

'Zola, can you believe it? I loved Thabo when he had nothing, *nothing*! But he wins a bit of money at the casino and suddenly he wants to leave me?' Zozo shouted.

Zola helped Zozo into a chair and got her a glass of water, which Zozo gulped down before immediately starting to howl again.

'Are you sure he broke up with you, Zozo?' Zola asked. 'What did he say?'

Zozo pulled her phone out of her bag and scrolled through Thabo's social media to find a post he'd made the night before. She showed Zola the screen.

It was him alright, dressed in tight acid-wash skinny jeans and an off-brand Uzzi T-shirt with his arm around a tall curvaceous woman in a short black dress. She was posed in an almost professional way while he stood with a goofy grin on his face.

Thabo had captioned the picture: *When you can afford better, you choose better.*

Zola scrolled up and down trying to find where he had said anything about breaking up with Zozo.

'Zo, where did he say anything about you?' Zola asked.

Zozo shook her head and snatched back her phone. 'He doesn't have to! He's supposed to be on a boys' trip to Krugersdorp. They went to a casino and he called me to tell me he'd won R100 000. Next thing, I see this post and now I can't get hold of him,' Zozo sobbed.

Zola took the phone and looked at the picture again. The woman was standing in front of a car with a large bow on it.

'Zozo, I think he just bought a car,' Zola said laughing. 'He didn't choose a new girl, Zozo – he chose a new *car!*'

Zozo snatched back the phone and zoomed into the picture, narrowing her eyes.

'That is a new car, isn't it?' Zozo sniffed. She flicked her finger over the screen and opened one of Thabo's friend's pages – there they were, all the guys piled into a second-hand Golf GTI, all grinning stupidly.

Zola smiled. 'Well, that was dramatic.'

Within minutes it was as if nothing had even happened. Zozo went into the bathroom to clean up while Zola called a taxi. When it arrived, they both climbed in, laughing and joking about how a crying Zozo had walked all the way over and it was all for nothing.

'Don't tell Thabo about any of this. I'll never hear the end of it,' Zozo laughed.

Zola envied how quickly Zozo got over things. Zozo didn't hide how she felt – she just let everything hang out, and she was happier for it.

Soon they had arrived at the new place Zola had seen online. They found a good spot and settled in to experience the vibe – it was just like it had seemed on the Instagram page, only with a lot more people, more noise and the smell of braai meat in the air.

'You've got something on you mind, Zola,' Zozo said as their cocktails arrived.

Zola stirred her drink with her straw. Thanks to Zozo's antics, she'd almost forgotten her troubles.

'Well, Okuhle called me today,' Zola started. 'I haven't seen her because she hasn't come to the office all week.' She sipped her drink.

Zozo leant forward, nodding.

'She told me everything. It turns out she and Mbali broke up years ago. She thought they were just on an extended break, but he was actually over the whole thing,' Zola said with a sigh.

'So now you can see where it goes with Mbali!' Zozo raised her hand for her signature high-five.

Zola pulled her hand down. 'No, it's more complicated than that. He was her first love and it's pretty clear to me that she still isn't over him. I can't get between them, not when she's my boss and I sit a few steps away from her for eight hours a day, five times a week.'

Zozo sighed in disappointment. 'Hhayi, Zola. Girls like Okuhle get everything. On the rare occasion that they don't, they throw woman-sized tantrums. Don't fall for it.'

Zola thought about it. Okuhle *had* said she wouldn't hold it against

Zola if she wanted to see where things went with Mbali. But would Mbali be interested in even talking to her now?

She shrugged. 'I guess I'll have to leave it to fate.'

Zozo was just about to start complaining about how Zola was too much of a good girl when a man stumbled and bumped into their table as he crashed to the ground.

'Watch it!' Zozo shouted.

'So sorry!' A familiar voice came from behind Zola and suddenly there was Mbali, helping the man up. He didn't seem to notice Zola.

'Mthunzi, you always do this, man. If I'd known you were in this state I wouldn't have come to pick you up. Now you're ruining these nice girls' lunch ...'

'Mbali?' Zola said in disbelief. What were the odds of bumping into the exact person she'd been talking about?

'Zola!' Mbali stopped.

They both looked at each other, not knowing what to say.

'This is *Mbali*?' Zozo smacked Zola's hand. 'Wow – can you believe that?'

'Ah, Mbali – this is my cousin, Zozo,' Zola introduced them. 'Zozo, Mbali.'

Mbali smiled at Zozo, his arms occupied with holding up Mthunzi.

'And this is my business partner, Mthunzi,' Mbali said, embarrassed.

Looking at Mthunzi too drunk to stand up, Zola cringed. 'Good thing I didn't get that job at *your* company.'

Mbali smiled and shook his head. 'Listen, are you staying here long? I'd really like to talk to you, Zola, but I first need to take this guy home.'

Zola hesitated but Zozo answered for her: 'Oh, no problem at all, Mbali. We'll *definitely* wait.'

Mbali winked before walking away and Zola felt her knees quiver.

'Cuz, you didn't tell me he was so sexy,' Zozo laughed as they watched Mbali struggle to get Mthunzi across the car park.

Zola rolled her eyes. She might not have told Zozo about his looks, but she had definitely noticed. She realised now that she'd even noticed at their failed interview how good-looking he was. And when he'd come by the office with flowers in hand, there'd been no mistaking that he looked like he'd just walked out of a catalogue for Big 'n Tall.

'You might deny it, but after seeing you literally drool when he winked, I know you like him too,' Zozo teased.

Zola wiped her chin, even though she was almost certain she hadn't actually drooled.

They chatted a while longer and then Zozo grabbed her phone and started scrolling, squinting through the blur caused by her two cocktails.

'What are you doing?' Zola asked.

'I'm asking Thabo to come get me,' Zozo laughed. 'He messaged a little while ago to say that he's back. I want to see his new car, and I want to give you and Mr Man some alone time.' She winked.

Mbali walked in just as Zozo was gathering her things.

'Nice meeting you, Mbali! Byee!' she said, making a face at Zola before she left.

'She's fun,' Mbali said.

'So much fun,' Zola agreed.

Mbali sat down, and they both waited for the other to speak.

'Look, I spoke to Okuhle,' Zola said eventually. 'And she told me everything.'

'She told me that too.'

'She's really hurt,' Zola said.

'I know.' Mbali looked down at his feet. 'It wasn't my intention to hurt her.'

Zola nodded. 'But you did.'

Mbali stared silently at Zola. He knew his mistakes better than she ever could, and she couldn't possibly make him feel any worse about Okuhle than he already did. But right now, the only feelings he was interested in hearing about were Zola's feelings for him – if she had any.

'I can't believe you're here,' Zola thought out loud. 'What are you even doing here?'

'I grew up not far from here in Turffontein.'

That was not where Zola had expected. She'd imagined Mbali as a gated-neighbourhood kind of guy, someone who'd grown up alongside a golf course or a lake or something.

'My parents travelled a lot for work. They were hardly ever around so I lived with my grandmother,' he explained.

Zola laughed. 'Is that where you get your taste for iskopo?'

'No, that comes from my uncle. He was a loan shark and he would take me to the taxi rank with him. Back then I thought he was the coolest guy in the world.' Mbali laughed.

So there really was more to him than just a cheese-boy living large on his dad's dime.

Zola smiled. 'You want to be a loan shark like your uncle?'

'I never wanted to be a loan shark – I don't have the stomach for it. But I did always want to be independent like my uncle, do my own thing, have a business to call my own.'

Zola nodded. She was aware that her heart was pounding and her nerves were singing just from being close to him. She felt every cell on her skin vibrate.

'Zola?' Mbali asked suddenly. 'What are we doing? I—'

Just at that moment the music was turned up. She couldn't hear what he was saying.

'What?' Zola leant in.

He saw her bring her head towards his, and with his eyes fixed on her face he leant in too, and pressed his lips against hers.

Zola's eyes closed at the unexpected pleasure. Heart racing, but with the taste of his kiss on her lips, Zola shifted back, away from Mbali.

'What did you say?' she asked breathlessly.

'I asked what we were doing, but I think I just got my answer.'

Chapter 24

The whirlwind

Zola's heart was still pounding when Mbali dropped her off outside her house.

'Leave quickly before Ma'Liphotho sees you,' she giggled.

'Or we could give her an actual show.' Mbali leant across the seats to kiss Zola again.

She closed her eyes and allowed herself to enjoy the kiss for a moment before pulling away.

'Maybe I should come say hello to your mother so she knows I'm not a dirty old man,' Mbali suggested.

'You're crazy,' Zola laughed, quickly jumping out of the car.

Mbali watched her skip away through the gate, and then she stood at the fence and watched him drive away.

She couldn't stop smiling. Even though she tried to act normal, she was still grinning stupidly when she came into the kitchen where her mother was washing the dishes.

'Zola, can I speak to you please?' Nomsebenzi asked.

Zola's mind shifted through the many things she could have done wrong. Had she left dishes in the sink? A mess in the bathroom? Should she have taken the chicken out of the freezer? Had she missed some unknown curfew?

She sat down at the kitchen table. Nomsebenzi sat down across from her and slid a set of keys across the table.

'You're a grown-up now, Zola. You've lived alone for many years, supported yourself and made your own decisions. I really hope you know right from wrong by now.'

Zola realised her mother was looking quite emotional.

'These are your keys, my girl. But I will still be locking my gate at seven.' Nomsebenzi got up and headed back to the sink.

Smiling inwardly, Zola took the keys and put them in her bag.

In their bedroom, Thobile was already fast asleep and Zola was free to feel as giddy as she wanted without an interrogation from her little sister. Singing, Zola walked back past her mother in the kitchen as she headed to the bathroom to get ready for bed.

Nomsebenzi laughed. 'Someone's happy. If I had known some keys would do that, I would have given them to you weeks ago.'

Zola smiled, not wanting to correct her mother and not wanting to tell her about Mbali just yet – not until she was sure what was going on between them.

Back in her bedroom, she checked her phone. A text from Mbali said that he'd arrived home safely and couldn't get her off his mind.

She couldn't get him off hers either.

Zola drifted off to sleep and didn't even feel guilty about not brushing her teeth before bed. She didn't want to scrub off Mbali's kiss, not just yet. She would savour the feeling of his soft lips on hers for as long as she could.

Zola woke up early in the morning and got ready for church even before her mother could say anything.

At finding her daughter waiting in the kitchen already dressed and ready, Nomsebenzi shook her head in amazement. 'Those really were some magical keys,' she said, mostly to herself.

'Well, it *is* Sunday, Ma,' Zola replied.

Thobile was also dressed for church, but was not as happy as her mother and sister, who chatted and sang all the way there.

When they arrived, Zola immediately spotted Zozo, who was wearing a bright-pink dress.

'Since when do *you* come to church?' Zozo whispered. 'Do you have some new sins that need forgiving?'

'Shh!' Zola hushed her with a finger on her lips. And for the next few hours she sat down, stood up, clapped and sang, but heard nothing of the sermon. While she usually got bored and started counting the hours till she could go home, thoughts of Mbali made the time fly, and before she knew it, the service was over and they were walking home.

Zola tried to keep up with her mother, who trotted quickly so she could get the pots on the stove ready for their late lunch. But turning the corner into their street, she immediately saw it in the distance outside their house.

Mbali's car. There was no mistaking it.

Zola's heart started to pound and she rushed ahead of Nomsebenzi so she could get to the house before her.

'What are you doing here?' Zola asked, catching her breath as she drew level with Mbali.

Mbali shrugged. 'I guess I'm here to meet your mother.'

Zola looked back but it was too late – her mother had already seen them. It was not like Mbali drove an inconspicuous car. And one thing was for sure: if Mbali left now, Nomsebenzi would definitely think the worst.

As they walked closer, Zola could see Thobile's eyes widen and her mouth fall open in comical shock. Her mother's face was harder to read.

'You're crazy,' Zola hissed at him.

Mbali smiled. 'I'm making your life easier. Trust me.'

'And what exactly are you going to introduce yourself as? My new boss's recent ex-boyfriend?'

'I thought we were over that?' Mbali said cheekily. 'What do you want me to introduce myself as?'

She blushed despite her irritation. 'I don't know …' Zola whispered. Her mother was now within earshot.

'Good afternoon, Ma,' Mbali greeted respectfully, extending his hand to shake Nomsebenzi's.

Nomsebenzi looked over at Zola and Zola looked at her shoes.

'Good afternoon,' Nomsebenzi said, shaking Mbali's hand. 'Let's get inside.'

Zola felt her breakfast rise from her stomach and threaten to make a reappearance right there on the street. She was sweating, and it wasn't because of the heat. Her armpits itched and she didn't know what to do with her hands.

They walked inside in silence. Her mother led the way to the living room and sat down on the single-seater couch. Zola wondered if she should sit next to Mbali or on the other couch.

'I'll get the juice,' she said instead, and walked off to the kitchen with Thobile following close behind her, her lips squeezed together in amusement.

'Wow – we're at meet-the-parents already?' Thobile giggled behind her hand.

Zola glared at her sister and got a tray ready with a jug of juice and glasses. She couldn't hear anything from the living room – her mother and Mbali were sitting in silence.

'Excuse me, I forgot something in the car,' she heard Mbali say.

Zola froze as he walked past her and out the door without a word. Was he *leaving*? But as she took the tray to the living room, she saw through the curtain that he was walking back in, this time with a cake in his hands.

'Ma,' he said as he re-emerged into the living room, 'I thought I should come and introduce myself so you don't have a stranger parked at your gate.' He offered Nomsebenzi the cake.

Nomsebenzi pressed her lips together and nodded. Zola knew that look – her mother was impressed.

'Yes, thank you. I have been wondering who it was that was bringing my daughter home so late,' Nomsebenzi said.

'I'm sorry I didn't come in sooner. I'm Mbali Thabethe, Ma. I'm Zola's boyfriend,' Mbali said.

My boyfriend? Zola thought she might drop the glass that she was about to pass to her mother.

'Oh, Mbali Thabethe,' Nomsebenzi repeated, looking over at Zola. 'Mbali is an odd name for a boy, isn't it?'

Zola glared at her mother and Thobile giggled.

Mbali smiled good-naturedly. 'Yes, I think so too. It's short for Mbalini, the name of the Congolese doctor who delivered me.'

Nomsebenzi laughed. 'I thought maybe you were just a really beautiful baby. Will you stay for lunch, Mbali? Zola just needs to get everything on the stove, then we can all have some of this lovely cake you've brought us. It's just what I felt like having today – it's as if you knew.'

Mbali winked at Zola as she got up to put the pots on the stove. 'Lunch would be great, thanks, Ma.'

From the kitchen minutes later, Zola could hear Mbali enthralling her mother with the story of how they had first met at the coffee shop, how Zola had clicked her tongue and stalked away, leaving him – her interviewer and prospective boss – gobsmacked at the table.

Nomsebenzi laughed and clapped her hands in a way neither Zola nor Thobile had heard for a long time.

'If you're not careful, Mom will steal your boyfriend,' Thobile sniggered as she brought the empty juice glasses to the kitchen.

THE THING WITH ZOLA

Zola listened as her mother and Mbali spoke about his childhood, Zola's childhood and a bunch of stories she had never heard from either of them.

One at a time Zola brought out plates of rice, pumpkin, beetroot and grilled chicken. She handed the plate with the drumstick she had been eyeing for herself to Mbali, another plate to her mother, and then she and Thobile sat down with their own plates.

Zola ate quietly while her mother and Mbali took turns telling stories about her and watching her blush.

After lunch was eaten and the cake was served, Mbali excused himself.

'Ma, I could sit here with you the whole night, but I have got to go. I have an early meeting in the morning.'

Nomsebenzi took Mbali's hand. 'Well, thank you for coming, Mbali. Gestures like this mean a lot to an old woman like me. You were raised well, and it shows.'

Zola walked Mbali out, still amazed at how he had charmed her mother.

'You know, you scare me,' she said leaning against the gate. 'I didn't think it was possible for anyone to make my mother so happy.'

Mbali shrugged. 'What can I say? I was raised right.' He kissed Zola on the cheek. 'By the way ... your mother is watching us from the window.'

Zola's eyes followed Mbali as he walked to the car and drove off.

'I like him,' Nomsebenzi told Zola as she walked back into the house. 'A very respectful boy.'

Zola was still on a high when she left for work early the next day, smiling to herself at the thought of Mbali, even though she had a long walk ahead of her in yet another downpour. She hopped across the street, jumping over puddles and dashing under the shelter of stores as she made her way through town and arrived at work still in high spirits.

Okuhle was there for a change, strapped up and bandaged but smiling.

'Hey, Zola, so glad you came in early,' Okuhle said, touching her arm. 'There are only four days till the expo and we have lots of details to finalise.'

She had somehow snapped back and was like the old Okuhle again. It would have made Zola nervous, except that she was in such a great mood.

'Some things have been delivered to the convention centre, and I was hoping you could come with me to have a look.'

Zola smiled back. 'Alright.'

'I still can't drive, so we'll have to take an Uber. I think we'll end up spending the day there, and then I'm going to head straight home, so maybe bring your stuff with you.'

It was still pouring outside when they left for the expo centre, sitting thigh to thigh in the back of the Uber, and it continued to rain throughout the day.

At the venue, the first thing they had to do was to check the set-up at the entrance. It was decorated African-style with proteas and sunflowers, animal hides and beads. A lot of the decorations they had been expecting hadn't arrived, but still it was breath-taking.

'Wow, this really is beautiful – it looks better than I imagined,' Zola gushed.

Inside, Zola carefully inspected a centrepiece at the sign-in table. She could never have imagined ostrich and peacock feathers not looking like a feather-duster, but among the reeds and the candles the feathery bouquet looked gorgeously glamorous.

'It is stunning, isn't it? This is the theme I would have wanted for my wedding …' Okuhle said as she whisked Zola into the main exhibition hall to check the tablecloths on the exhibitors' stands.

Zola flinched. Was it her fault that wasn't going to happen for Okuhle?

She knew that technically it wasn't, but still …

Standing in an archway of what looked like very large elephant tusks, Okuhle was perfectly framed, even with her arm in a sling, her hair combed out like a halo around her face. If there was any sadness in her face, it flickered past quickly – so quickly that Zola missed it completely.

'Anyway, at least I can still enjoy my big day – even if it's at an expo rather than a wedding,' Okuhle said brightly.

Okuhle knocked on the tusks as if to make sure they weren't real and then set off to inspect another harvest-table-themed centrepiece, sniffing at the real fruit and veggies that had been laid out artfully on the table. *Her boss certainly didn't miss a beat,* thought Zola.

Later in the afternoon, Zola was using her phone to take pictures of bejewelled headpieces in their glass display cases when a message arrived from Mbali.

It's pouring. I'll take you home.

Perfect – Okuhle had already said she'd need to find her own lift, and a trip in a dry car beat a crowded taxi any day. Zola quickly sent a reply, telling Mbali where she was.

'What do you think about these umbrellas as a party favour?' Okuhle asked, opening an umbrella and dancing a few steps. 'They're gorgeous aren't they?'

With all the excitement of seeing what they had been working so hard for, both their heads were buzzing.

'Right, Zola, I think we can call it a day,' Okuhle said a little while later. 'I'm exhausted. Can I call you a cab?'

'That's okay, I'll be fine,' Zola said.

Okuhle hesitated as she read between the lines. 'Okay. Well, I'm off then.'

Mbali arrived not long after, and Zola was grateful that Okuhle had left already – an awkward encounter had been avoided. Sheltering at the entrance, Zola watched as Mbali climbed out of the car, dodging the rain, and ran to greet her. Despite her protestations that she was fine, he insisted on putting his jacket over her head as they prepared to run back to the car.

'Oh! Hi, Mbali.'

And there was Okuhle, suddenly standing in the doorway of the expo centre. 'Sorry, I … I forgot a file …' she said, touching an A4 manila envelope.

'Okuhle, we don't need to avoid each other,' Mbali said.

Zola's eyes met with Okuhle's, and she looked away, yet again feeling a pang of guilt.

'Yes, actually, it seems we really do.' Okuhle's smile didn't quite reach her eyes. 'At least … for a little while longer.'

As Mbali slid into the car and they drove off in silence, only Zola seemed to notice Okuhle was still standing watching them, mascara running down her face like tears.

Chapter 25

Tormented

Zola came into work the next day with a heaviness that was in direct contrast with the lightness she'd been feeling since her and Mbali's kiss. Seeing Okuhle so cut up about Mbali made her feel terrible. She felt like a thief, like she'd stolen Okuhle's happiness.

Okuhle was already sitting at her desk while all around her, men in overalls were taking down her paintings, the flower wall behind her desk and even some of the cabinets.

Zola looked in curiously. 'Morning, Okuhle. Is everything okay?'

'Yip,' Okuhle said, getting up from her chair and examining the piles of items arranged all over her desk. She picked up a watch with beautiful sparkling gemstones in different colours all along the band. 'With all this focus on the expo I realised I needed to pay some attention to my own space. So I'm just getting rid of some old junk. You know. Bad memories.'

'That's gorgeous,' said Zola. 'Why are you throwing it away?'

'Oh, you can have it – and anything else you want from that pile. I want a fresh start.'

Zola looked over the pile. There were some lovely things, but she didn't feel comfortable taking anything apart from the watch. She strapped it on her wrist – it did seem to suit her – and sat down at her desk ready to work. She read through her emails and tried to keep herself from looking over at Okuhle, who seemed preoccupied with throwing things out.

'I think the carpet needs to go too,' Okuhle announced to the workmen. 'Yes, take the carpet, please.'

Zola watched as more of the staff were invited into Okuhle's office to browse through her growing pile of castoffs.

'What's up with your boss?' Khanyisa asked settling in. 'I thought she'd be all about the expo this week, but I've just got this awesome vase and an unopened box of Belgian chocolates. The admin girls are all fighting over some of Okuhle's earrings.'

Zola raised her shoulders in a shrug. 'Apparently she's starting over.'

Zola wasn't sure what it was about, but she was certain she didn't want to know any more than she had to.

Khanyisa laughed. 'I always knew she'd lose it.'

'Hey, don't say that,' Zola leapt to Okuhle's defence. 'She's obviously just going through something.'

Khanyisa rolled her eyes and started up her laptop while Zola watched Okuhle carry more ornaments out of the bathroom with her one functional arm, struggling through obvious pain. Zola knew it wasn't her place to help, but she really wanted to. She hated to see Okuhle like this. It only made her guilt heavier to bear.

'You know, maybe we should move to a new office space all together,' Okuhle said loudly from the passage.

The cleaning spree went on the whole day. She didn't answer emails or her phone. With the expo just three days away, Zola was worried.

'Um, Okuhle?' Zola said coming into the messy office towards the end of a less-than-productive afternoon. 'I've sent you an email with things you need to approve. It's kind of urgent.'

Okuhle turned and glared at Zola. 'Oh, so you're the boss now? You're going to tell me what to do?' She raised her voice. 'I'll respond to your emails when I damn well feel like it!'

The office fell silent, and Zola stood stunned. Then Okuhle turned and walked away like nothing had happened.

Zola felt a lump in her throat and blinked away the tears. She walked sheepishly back to her desk and sat down.

'Sorry,' Khanyisa whispered. 'I did warn you though. Okuhle is totally nuts.'

For the next hour, Zola kept her head down and tried to pick up Okuhle's slack until it was time to go. When Khanyisa got up to leave at exactly five o'clock, Zola did the same.

Zola got home feeling drained. She didn't want to eat, and she hardly said a word to her mother or her sister. She just wanted to take a bath and go to bed.

She called Mbali to say goodnight, and he knew from her voice that something was wrong.

'She did *what*?' he asked angrily after Zola had recounted the story of her day.

'I'm not telling you this so you can do something about it,' Zola said. 'I'm just telling you what happened.'

'But she can't treat you that way,' Mbali argued, clearly livid. 'You were just doing your job. And she needed to do hers.'

From the thudding sound coming through the phone, Zola could tell he was pacing.

'She'll get over it.' Zola suddenly became the comforter, even though she had called to be comforted. 'I guess we just have to give her time.'

Mbali stopped pacing. 'I guess so,' he agreed. 'But if she ever does anything like that again, I'm going to have to do something about it.'

Zola giggled. 'I like how protective you are.'

'I thought you were upset.'

'I was until I spoke to you.'

'I'm glad I could cheer you up. Listen, my dad's back from Tokyo and I'm seeing him on Thursday so I might need some cheering up myself afterwards. Meet me for dinner?'

'I've got the expo the next day, but I suppose everyone has to eat. Pick me up after work?'

'Right at the gate.'

Zola fell asleep feeling a lot better.

Except for Okuhle, the office was empty as usual when Zola arrived on Thursday morning. Wednesday had passed in a blur of activity. She'd had to pick up a lot of Okuhle's slack, but everything was now sorted and Zola was feeling good about the expo. She could afford to take a little breather tonight, and she was looking forward to seeing Mbali for dinner. Although she hadn't mentioned her date to Nomsebenzi, Zola had come in dressed for her date with Mbali – a tight black dress, nothing too fancy, but with her new watch strapped to her wrist and a set of matching bangles.

When she saw Zola arrive, Okuhle sheepishly walked out of her office and set a beautifully wrapped box of chocolates on Zola's desk.

'I'm sorry,' she said.

Zola looked up at her and nodded.

'I saw the emails you've been sending, and I realise I've dropped the ball. I've been—' Okuhle paused to choose her next words. 'Anyway, thank you for holding the fort.'

'It's okay,' Zola said shortly to avoid a full-blown conversation with Okuhle. She had just wanted a normal work life, but it was becoming obvious that it was impossible with a boss like Okuhle.

'I broke my promise. I let things that have nothing to do with work affect our working relationship, and I'll do better from here on.' Okuhle left the chocolates on Zola's desk and went back to her own.

Zola moved the box aside and started her day. She went through her emails, realising she would still have to sit down with Okuhle to brief her on some last details.

On the other side of the glass, in her now-bare office, Okuhle sat feeling sorry for herself. Changing the décor had been quite a rush, but now she was faced with that awkward feeling of emptiness where the old vision had been removed but her new vision had not yet taken shape. She'd wanted to purge herself of everything that reminded her of Mbali and the life she thought they'd have, but even in this empty office she hadn't been able to rid herself of him.

Eventually she picked up the phone and called her mother.

'Hlehle, darling, how's the expo coming? I'm so excited to see what you've done!'

'Yeah, everything is great,' Okuhle replied, her tone dull.

'Baby, what's wrong?' Priscilla sighed. 'Please don't tell me this is about Mbali. I am so tired of hearing about that boy.'

Okuhle got up to close the door to her office. The empty walls and floors now irritated her more than the office she had decorated with Mbali. It was yet another reminder that the happy times were over.

'You're obsessed with that boy, Okuhle, and it's not healthy. I'm going to be straight with you because I'm your mother and I care about you. You need to stop this now,' Priscilla lectured.

Okuhle groaned into the phone. 'You don't understand, Mama. It's harder than you think.'

But Priscilla was not having it – she was tired of Okuhle's constant complaining and scheming, and she was becoming seriously worried about her daughter. 'You are not the first woman to have her heart broken, Okuhle. And like everyone else, you'll get over it.'

Okuhle tried to protest, but her mother cut her off.

'No, baby, people get over the end of marriages that have lasted their entire adult lives – and you want to fall apart over your high-school boyfriend? There's nothing you can do to make him marry you,' Priscilla said firmly. 'And there's nothing I can do either.'

'Geez, Mom, I'm not asking you to.'

Hearing what her mother thought of the situation really did make her sound crazy and sitting in the stripped-down office only drove that message home.

'If I knew how to just get over him, I would,' Okuhle said. 'In a heartbeat.'

She looked through her glass wall at Zola, who was sitting at her desk as calm as a cucumber. *Let's not forget*, Okuhle thought to herself, *that Zola had also just gotten out of a long-term relationship*.

'Start dating again,' Priscilla suggested. 'There's even online dating. There are so many men out there, many of them a lot better than Mbali.'

Okuhle laughed at the idea at first, but it didn't take long for Priscilla's suggestion to start making sense.

'Thank you for the pep talk, Mom,' Okuhle said. 'I needed to hear that.'

'I'll see you tomorrow for the expo, baby – and I can't wait to see what you've done!'

As soon as she'd cut the call, Okuhle began scrolling through her phone, picking out her favourite pictures to create an online dating profile. Sure, things were busy at the office, but if she could afford twelve people's salaries, she could surely afford a little me-time? Whatever came up, she was sure Zola could handle it.

It didn't take Okuhle long to set up her new dating profile.

She posted just enough basic information to let her swipe through the profiles of the men who, like her, were looking for love on the Internet, and she spent a short while flipping through one profile after another. Nothing piqued her interest, but less than an hour after she'd gone online, she received a notification: her first message.

Okuhle was excited. She looked around the office to check if anyone could see what she was doing, but everyone's heads were down.

The message was from someone called Leruo. He didn't have a profile picture, but he was apparently a lecturer at the University of Johannesburg. Not too far from her.

Hi Okuhle
Did you by any chance go to St Phillipe's School in the south of Johannesburg?
Best,
Leruo

Okuhle frowned. She had been to St Phillipe's, but this Leruo seemed to think he knew her, and his name didn't ring a bell. Horror stories about online stalkers-turned-murderers flashed in her mind, but Leruo sent another message just as Okuhle was second-guessing her decision.

I used to go by Malikhai at school. I was a year ahead of you.

Now there was a picture attached, a vaguely familiar face. A handsome man with long dreadlocks tied in a bun at the top of his head, a dusting of freckles on his cheeks and a thick beard. Okuhle decided to text back.

You look kind of familiar, but it's weird that you don't have a profile picture.

Leruo was on the ball. He responded before Okuhle could decide if she should delete her profile.

Students can be mean. Just avoiding having screenshots of my profile floating around campus.

Okuhle laughed – campus sounded brutal. Yes, she thought she did remember a Malikhai from high school. He'd been small and reedy, but it looked like he'd filled out. Even from his headshot she could see broad shoulders, the top of his chiselled pecs pressing against his shirt.

Okuhle was definitely interested, but this was awkward. How to start a conversation with an old acquaintance on an online dating site? She stuck to the script she always used after bumping into old acquaintances.

So, what have you been up to? Haven't seen or heard about you since school.

This time Leruo didn't reply quite so fast. Okuhle watched her screen, repetitively refreshing the page until a message came through.

Can we catch up over coffee? Still new to this online-dating thing and it's really awkward.

Okuhle thought about it. She was also nervous, but it helped that she was talking to someone she already kind of knew.

Sure. Busy preparing for an expo I'm organising for most of tomorrow. Maybe come and meet me there? I'm sure I can disappear for a coffee.

Leruo agreed and sent Okuhle his number asking her to let him know the details, and Okuhle felt a whole swarm of butterflies fluttering inside her.

When that was done, she got up to get herself a cup of coffee just as Zola walked out of the office to leave for the day.

'Bye, Zola,' Okuhle chimed.

'Bye, Okuhle,' Zola called.

In the quiet office, Okuhle made her coffee and walked back to her desk. Passing near Zola's desk, she saw the chocolates she'd given her, untouched. Thinking she might still catch her, she grabbed the box and looked out of the window.

Outside, Zola was getting into Mbali's car. Okuhle moved back away from the window, hoping that the stabbing pain in her chest would dull down as she moved on too.

Chapter 26

The rebound

Zola walked out of the office in her booty-hugging black dress. Her strappy stiletto heels clicked across the pavement as she swayed her hips. She'd put up with minor discomfort from her outfit all day just for this moment. She knew Mbali was watching her – she could clearly see him through the car's windscreen. She flipped her hair seductively. Judging by the reaction from her audience of one, the forty-five minutes she'd spent laying down her edges and straightening her new wig had been worth it.

Biting his lip, Mbali stepped out of the car and walked around to open Zola's door. She slid into her seat and gave Mbali a quick kiss.

'Hi.' She smiled, taking in his reaction.

'You look gorgeous,' Mbali said still taking Zola in. 'As usual.'

At the next red light he leant over and kissed her hand, moving up her arm and slowly around the back of her neck until they were interrupted by a chorus of hooting cars.

'I think you should focus on the road,' Zola laughed, feeling a flush of heat through her body.

The drive was short, even through peak evening traffic, and before long they had arrived at the Michelangelo Hotel in Sandton, a place Zola had only seen online. They walked up the stairs, hand in hand. Zola was surprised by how soft Mbali's hands were.

'Good choice for a first date,' she said, admiring the hotel's beauty.

'*First* date? More like third.'

'Not every meal is a date, you know. And it doesn't count if we weren't actually dating at the time.' Zola grinned. 'So this is the first *official* date.'

Mbali shook his head and wrapped his hand around Zola's waist. 'You're just being difficult.' Ever so lightly, with every step they took, his hand caressed the curve of her buttocks.

Zola walked slower as they moved towards their table, enjoying the closeness of their bodies.

'Madame.' Mbali bowed dramatically as he pulled out Zola's chair.

She smiled. 'Thank you, sir.'

A waitress soon arrived at the table and handed them their menus. Zola reached to take hers and noticed Mbali's face change.

'Where did you get that?' he asked, his brow furrowed, as he looked at her wrist.

Zola followed his eyes to her beautiful new watch. 'From Okuhle,' she said. 'She's redecorating her office and she thought I'd like this. I do.'

Mbali's nostrils flared. 'Take it off,' he said, reaching over to take it. 'Please.'

'Why?'

'Because I'd like to have one date without her meddling. Please … give me the watch.'

Zola was confused, but reluctantly gave it up. Mbali angrily pushed it into his shirt pocket.

'You two have too many secrets,' Zola said irritably.

'I bought her that watch,' Mbali said, signalling for the waitress to return to the table. 'I'd like a double shot of Johnnie Walker – Black if you have it. No ice. What would you like, Zola?'

'A Long Island iced tea, please,' Zola said without looking at the waitress. She couldn't hide how upset she was. She knew Okuhle had given her the watch on purpose – just another way to insert herself into Mbali's life, force him to think of her even when he was alone with Zola. She sat pouting, her arms folded over her chest.

'I think I should start job hunting again,' Zola announced. 'This isn't going to work.'

'I won't argue with that.' Mbali took his drink from the waitress and gulped it down. He sighed and visibly relaxed.

'I just want you to be happy, Zola.'

Zola was determined to be happy too. She wanted to be deliriously happy, but right now she was wondering if she could ever be happy with Mbali, because with Mbali there would always be Okuhle, and Okuhle was more baggage than Zola could handle.

'So … Industrial engineering is a unique choice. Why did you choose that of all things?'

Mbali's question came out of the blue. 'Are you making up for the interview you refused to give me?'

Mbali laughed. 'Firstly, I never refused you an interview. And secondly, I'm just trying to get to know you better. And so far, you've been very evasive.'

Zola nodded. She'd heard that before. She wasn't easy to get to know, she didn't make friends easily and there were very few people she genuinely liked.

'Well, I chose industrial engineering because I wanted to live overseas and live the life I wanted to live instead of the life I could afford,' Zola said honestly.

'And if it wasn't about money, what would you have done?'

Zola cleared her throat. 'I've never thought about that because I've never been in a position where it wasn't about money.'

This was something Zola knew Mbali wouldn't understand. He'd never had to feel that choking anxiety over the future, the fear that things might get a lot worse than just today's struggles. She knew he'd never had to think before he spent. And knowing that he didn't understand what she was talking about made Zola uneasy.

Mbali didn't seem to have noticed her discomfort. He just looked at Zola in silence for longer than Zola was comfortable with.

'What?' Zola laughed blushing. 'Is there something on my face?'

'No,' Mbali said smiling. 'You have so many layers, it's like I meet a different version of you every day.'

'Rich people romanticise everything,' Zola said dismissively.

'I'm not "rich people". My parents are rich people, but I have a start-up that hasn't even started yet.'

Zola rolled her eyes at Mbali's attempt to lighten the mood. 'It appears we're at the what's-your-favourite-colour stage of the date,' she said lightly.

'I guess we are.' But he seemed distracted as he looked at a man walking towards a table behind Zola.

She turned to see an older man pulling out a chair for a young woman dressed in a short neon-pink cocktail dress, with a peroxide blonde wig and matching complexion. She was doll-like, tottering on too-high heels behind her much older companion. Zola might have thought they were a father and daughter, except that the old man was practically salivating as he leered at his date.

'Do you know them?' Zola asked.

Mbali nodded slowly. 'That's my dad.'

Zola noticed that Mbali looked angry and ashamed all at once.

The young woman looked no older than a teenager, and she was clearly not Mbali's mother.

'Do you want to leave?' Zola asked quietly.

THE THING WITH ZOLA

'In a moment.' Mbali pushed back his chair and made his way to his father in quick, angry strides.

Zola watched on, not knowing what to expect. Tactfully, she called over the waitress and asked for the bill. From across the crowded restaurant she could hear Mbali and his father's heated conversation.

'Baba, is this what you're doing now?'

Elias looked more irritated than ashamed. 'Don't come here acting all high and mighty, Mbali. Me and you are doing the exact same thing in the exact same place. Just go sit down.'

'I'm not doing anything like what you're doing,' Mbali hissed. 'I'm having dinner with my girlfriend.'

Elias leant back and exhaled loudly. 'That girl is not your girlfriend. At the most she's a rebound,' he said loudly. 'I know you, you pretend to be righteous Mr Clean, when in reality you just want things to be easy. Okuhle makes things easy and when you're done showing off, you'll crawl back to her.' Elias laughed.

'You know nothing about me,' Mbali fumed. 'And no, we are not the same!' Mbali stormed back towards Zola.

Zola was stunned. Mbali had told her that he had a difficult relationship with his father, but she had never imagined something like this. After Mbali had fumbled for his wallet to pay the bill, she got up to follow him out of the hotel, turning back to see Mbali's father calmly continuing with his date.

Mbali was walking too fast, and Zola had to trot to keep up. They crossed the car park to the Chevrolet, where Mbali threw open her car door and moved around to his side before Zola had even reached it.

Once in the car, Zola found Mbali breathing hard, his fingers tightly gripping the steering wheel.

'I'm sorry about that,' he said with control.

Zola felt sorry for him. It wasn't his fault his father had chosen the same restaurant as them.

'You really have nothing to be sorry about,' Zola said. 'I much prefer

McDonald's anyway.'

Moments later, Mbali swung the car past the golden arches into the drive-through.

'My treat,' Zola said. 'As a feminist, I insist on paying for our second official date.'

After they'd picked up their order, Mbali parked the car.

'Tell me anything,' Mbali said between sips of his Coke as the awkwardness of seeing Elias slowly dissipated.

Zola took a moment. She dismissed saying anything about work – Okuhle was not welcome here. Zola couldn't speak about her mother because that would only make Mbali think of *his* mother – and then his father. And Zola definitely couldn't speak about her time in Germany, because everything about Munich somehow related to Günter.

'So … Matshepo is finally pregnant. I'm so happy for her after all the drama with her baby-daddy. *He's* a piece of work.'

Mbali raised a curious eyebrow. 'One of your friends?'

'What? No! One of the Housewives – Zozo watches it religiously and now I'm hooked too!' Zola laughed scrolling through her phone to find Matshepo's Instagram.

By the time she'd caught Mbali up on reality TV, her guilty pleasure, and the shenanigans of her favourite onscreen pals, some hours had passed – and neither she nor Mbali could wait for the next episode.

'If we extend this dinner any later we'll get in trouble with your mom,' he said looking at the time on his dashboard.

'I don't want to go home,' Zola said, leaning over and kissing Mbali gently. She bit his bottom lip as she deepened the kiss, her hand stroking the back of his head.

'You sure?' Mbali asked.

'I'm sure.'

Chapter 27

Frenemies

Waking up on Friday morning in Mbali's apartment, Zola realised how impulsive she had been. Flashes of the night before came to her in short, toe-curling bursts as she took in Mbali's stylish apartment in the morning light.

Thankfully, she'd remembered to text her mother to say that she was working late, that she'd only be done after the last taxis had left so she'd sleep at the home of a colleague – she knew Nomsebenzi wouldn't argue if it was work-related.

But still, Zola knew she'd been reckless – today was the expo, and she hadn't given a thought to what she'd wear to it.

'Shit!' she whispered, jumping out of Mbali's futon bed. It fit perfectly with the minimalistic style of the apartment, but for all its sophistication and cloud-like softness, it was a pain to get out of.

'What? What's wrong?' Mbali woke up quickly and sat up, the thin silk sheet sliding off his body.

He sat rubbing the sleep from his eyes, completely confident in his nakedness. *Definitely a king in his castle*, Zola thought – everything in the apartment seemed designed specifically for him. It was all sleek and tidy, in shades of grey and white. Simple, crisp and clean.

Zola was already putting on yesterday's black dress and brushing down the edges of her neat cornrows.

'Where are you going? Come back to bed.'

Zola looked at him in wide-eyed panic. 'I don't have anything to wear to work today!'

Mbali lay back down on his pillows, his hands behind his head. 'And what exactly are you planning to do about that at five o'clock in the morning?'

Zola sat back down on the bed with her head in her hands. 'You aren't even trying to help me ...'

Mbali tapped the bed with his hand. 'Come on. I'll make a plan for you, and you'll be your usual gorgeous self at work. No walk of shame necessary.'

'But the wedding expo starts in four hours' time,' Zola said, flopping onto her back to stare at the ceiling.

'And I'm sure it'll be a raving success,' Mbali said as he rolled over to take Zola's hand. He kissed it. 'More importantly ... last night was incredible.' He pulled her close.

Zola smiled. 'It was, wasn't it.'

'Now go back to sleep. You have a big day ahead of you,' Mbali said sleepily. 'And you don't have to commute all the way from Vosloorus this morning.'

Zola closed her eyes but couldn't fall back asleep.

She was stressed about the expo and wished Mbali could be there to support her. But that would be a disaster. Both Okuhle and her mother would be there, and Zola didn't want to imagine the fireworks if he pitched up.

She lay in Mbali's arms until his alarm went off two hours later. Normally she would have already been on a taxi by now, and on her way to joining the snaking line for her second.

'Good morning,' Mbali whispered, kissing her neck. His hands moved over her body, caressing. Zola groaned in response, but self-control won and she moved out of his reach and climbed out of bed.

'What's your plan? I have to be at the office in two hours,' she said.

'And the shops open in one hour,' Mbali replied. 'Tell me what you'd like to wear today.'

Half an hour later, freshly showered and dressed in one of Mbali's loose-fitting tracksuits, Zola was sitting anxiously in Mbali's car.

'Why do you look so worried?' he asked.

'I have to go to the expo dressed in this?' She pulled at the baggy pants.

'That's my favourite tracksuit!' Mbali complained. 'Besides, I said I'll sort that out, and I will. Trust me.'

Mbali drove past the robots he should have turned at to get to the Larger Than Life offices, and headed towards Hyde Park. Once there, he parked outside a small boutique store.

'And here we are! All the clothes you could ever want! I told you, Zo – I've got you.'

Zola leant over excitedly and kissed Mbali before jumping out of the car. Mbali walked into the boutique behind her.

Having just opened, the store was quiet and Zola had it all to herself. She looked through the racks of clothing waiting for something to catch her eye.

'What about this?' Mbali said, showing Zola a floral A-line dress.

'It's cute, very sixties,' Zola said, still looking around.

'I thought you were worried about being late?' Mbali offered Zola the same dress again.

'Yes, fine ... I'll be back.' She headed to the change room and pulled on the dress.

It fit perfectly and was just her style – it even worked with the shoes she'd worn the night before.

'Mbali, it's perfect,' she squealed, dancing out of the fitting rooms. 'I look like a wedding guest – just the look I was going for.'

The sales lady quickly came round from behind the counter with the card machine.

'We only had two of these in stock, and the other one sold yesterday. You're lucky you got here early – it would have been gone by lunch time.'

By the time Zola arrived at the office she felt great, sure everything would go perfectly.

She walked in to find an older woman who looked vaguely familiar standing at the coffee station. Even though Zola knew she'd seen the woman somewhere before, she couldn't place her.

'You must be Zola,' the woman said, looking her up and down.

Zola took a moment to try and remember how they might know each other.

'Oh, we've never met,' the woman said. Her unsmiling face suggested she had an axe to grind, but if they'd never met, it was hard to figure out why.

'It appears you have the same taste as my daughter,' the woman said, shaking her head. 'I'm Minister Priscilla Msimanga, Okuhle's mother,' she said, not holding out her hand for Zola to shake.

'Nice to meet you,' Zola said, smoothing her dress and wondering what on earth the minister could mean.

'Oh my gosh! I can't believe it! Twins!' Coming out of her office, Okuhle squealed a pasted-on clown smile that threatened to split her face. She was wearing exactly the same dress as Zola!

Zola's eyes widened. Of all the people in Johannesburg, it had to be Okuhle who'd bought the only other dress!

THE THING WITH ZOLA

'Yay. Twins,' Zola said, not quite matching Okuhle's apparent pleasure.

'You've met my mother?' Okuhle said indicating the older woman, who nodded curtly. 'Good, let's get going then. I can't wait for you all to see what the decorators have done. I was there yesterday,' Okuhle gushed. 'I was gobsmacked!'

Zola walked behind Okuhle and Priscilla to the minister's smart black SUV, and climbed into the back seat. From the front, Okuhle chattered for a while about the event, the food and a man called Leruo.

Out of nowhere, Priscilla sucked her teeth. 'I'm so glad you're rid of that good-for-nothing leech.'

'Mama!' Okuhle said, apologetically looking back at Zola.

'Oh, she'll see for herself sooner rather than later,' Priscilla continued.

So maybe it wasn't just the dress Priscilla had been referring to when she'd said they shared the same taste – Okuhle must have told her mother about Zola and Mbali.

Zola sat uncomfortably in her seat, looking out of the window. Occasionally Priscilla looked back at her through the rear-view mirror, almost as if she was checking on her, expecting her to be stealing something from the back seat of the car. There was something frightening about the woman – she exuded power and confidence and seemed to wield it like a sledgehammer.

'So, Zola, were you expecting blue lights?' Priscilla suddenly snorted. 'That's the problem with you people. You complain about how other people live until you get the chance to taste that life. But I'll tell you something about me – something you'll never read in any newspaper. I've had my fill of struggle, and I won't stomach inconvenience. I won't wait for any driver, I won't be jostled about by nobodies in black suits. So I do what I want, and today I want to drive my baby girl to work.'

It was the most uncomfortable ten minutes of Zola's life, and she heaved a sigh of relief when they finally arrived at the expo centre. She should have gone straight there, she realised – she hadn't needed to arrive with Okuhle, and she would have preferred to avoid being anywhere near Okuhle's mother.

'I have a phone call to make. I'll see you girls inside,' Priscilla said dismissively, having parked the car.

'I'm really sorry about my mom,' Okuhle said squeezing Zola's hand as they walked towards the entrance.

'Don't worry about it.' Zola felt odd walking hand in hand with Okuhle in matching dresses, but was still too terrified of Priscilla to say anything.

Once inside the foyer, Zola could see that Okuhle was right: the hall had been completely transformed, and it was beautiful. For all her weird behaviour, Okuhle really did know how to pull off a spectacular event, and although it was not what she'd ever thought she'd be doing with her life, Zola could feel the thrill of being involved in a big splash like this. If she was being honest, there were many times she'd worried they wouldn't pull it off, but they'd created something beautiful. The thrill of achievement surged through Zola's body.

She took a deep breath and stepped into the fray.

And for the rest of the day, she barely came up for air.

Late that afternoon, Zola was at the back-area kitchen talking to the caterers when Priscilla came up to her. She casually poked around at the leftover dishes on the countertop.

'You know, Zola, despite all the other nonsense you kids have been getting up to, I'm really impressed.'

Zola wasn't sure how to react.

'Thank you,' Zola said, hoping that was the end of that conversation.

It wasn't.

'And despite where we both are in our lives right now, in many ways we are more similar to each other than either of us is to Okuhle,' she said slowly and deliberately. 'I've coddled her. Sure, she works hard, but it

THE THING WITH ZOLA

helps that I can pull strings for her,' Priscilla admitted. 'But like me, *you* work for everything you have, and you work hard. I've seen your CV. For a woman your age, you've done well.'

Zola felt awkward. She had no idea where this was going.

'I mean, from Vosloorus to Munich all by yourself, collecting distinction after distinction in a foreign country while probably suffering culture shock and homesickness. Really, your mother must be proud.'

'She is, thank you.' Zola hoped to find a hole in the conversation where she could excuse herself.

'It will be interesting to see how far you go. You could be anything. *Anything*.' Priscilla smiled. It wasn't a happy smile – it was a practised smile. 'And that's another difference between you and Okuhle. Okuhle is already set up to succeed. She has no choice in the matter. Everything has already been worked out and even if she does the bare minimum, she'll go far.'

Zola was growing impatient. Priscilla's monologue didn't seem to be going anywhere, and Zola had things to do.

'Okuhle and Mbali are the same. Mbali is rebelling right now, trying to prove a point to his asshole father. He wants to run his business his way, bring home a girl who will embarrass Elias and just act out in every way he can.'

Priscilla's point was finally becoming clear. Zola stared blankly at her, not wanting to give her the satisfaction of a reaction.

Priscilla laughed. 'This fun new relationship of yours is part of one long, bratty tantrum. Now, because you are so much like me and because I like you, Zola – really, I do – I thought I'd give you some motherly advice.' Priscilla put her hand on Zola's shoulder, her face full of concern.

Zola could hear her heartbeat in her ears. She wanted to shrug Priscilla's hand off her shoulder, but she couldn't move.

'Don't do this to yourself, baby. You're smart, you're beautiful and there are thousands of men out there who would be just perfect for you. Mbali is not one of them. In the end, he'll go back to Okuhle, and you'll be left out in the cold. And that's not the worst part of it, you know? Think of all the bridges you will have burnt.'

It became terrifyingly clear to Zola where Okuhle got her duality from – right now, Priscilla had the same fake smile Okuhle had worn when she'd first seen Zola and Mbali eating lunch outside her office. Priscilla was just more vicious than her daughter.

'He's not worth it, baby.'

Zola watched Priscilla turn and walk away. She finally saw the security the minister had said she didn't need. Five men with headsets hanging from their ears followed her swiftly out the door.

As the expo came to a close, everyone involved was on a high – and the initial feedback had been excellent. Zola bumped into Okuhle just as the final exhibitors were packing up.

She and Okuhle hadn't actually seen much of each other over the course of the day – although Zola had spied her boss sitting at the coffee shop, once with her mother, and once with a man with long dreadlocks, laughing as if she didn't have a care in the world.

'Wow, Okuhle, this has been amazing,' Zola said. 'Seriously, you've outdone yourself.'

'No, Zola, *we've* outdone ourselves. Even with everything that's been going on, you've had my back all the way with this event. I'm so proud of us.' Okuhle hugged Zola tightly, and although Zola hesitated at first, she finally succumbed. Okuhle was right – as far as the expo was concerned, they really had worked well together.

'And that's why I'm excited to tell you about our next opportunity – I can't even wait till Monday!' Okuhle carried on excitedly. 'My mother showed some delegates from Africa around this expo, and they want to take it further. We've got a new contract and I've already signed the paperwork! Zola, I want you to represent Larger Than Life. In Rwanda.'

Chapter 28

A time for romance

Zola woke up on Saturday morning feeling weighed down. The expo had gone off without a hitch, but she was exhausted, and Priscilla's clear threat kept playing back in Zola's mind. It was one thing being told off by her boss's mother, but this mother was a government minister with a security detail to boot. On top of that was Okuhle's Rwanda idea. And while Zola liked the idea of travel – and maybe it was even a promotion – she wasn't sure of Okuhle's motives. Or Priscilla's, for that matter.

Also, Zola had always imagined her life happening in Europe. She'd prepared herself for snowy winters and the strain of having to do her own hair. Was Rwanda really her Plan B? From industrial engineer to event manager … She didn't have much time to think about it because before she'd properly opened her eyes, her phone rang.

Mbali.

'Morning! I have a surprise for you to celebrate your success,' he said.

'Pack an overnight bag and be ready in two minutes.'

'Where are you?'

'Outside your gate.'

'I don't like surprises,' Zola pouted, climbing into Mbali's car ten minutes later.

She'd left a note for Nomsebenzi saying that she'd left to pack up at the expo and would be staying at a colleague in Randburg overnight. She didn't like lying to her mother, but Nomsebenzi would never stomach her going on a night away with Mbali, however much she liked him.

'I mean, how am I supposed to prepare if you won't tell me where we're going and what we are going to do there?'

Mbali started the car and swung it into the road with just a smile in response. They pulled onto the freeway and as he drove faster, he tapped the steering wheel to the rhythm of a song on the radio.

'You're going the wrong way,' Zola warned.

Mbali didn't flinch. 'No, we're not. And you don't even know where we're going,' he laughed.

Zola sighed. Exactly what kind of baecation was this?

Mbali smiled, rubbing the back of his hand over Zola's cheek. 'All you have to worry about this weekend was what you had to tell your mother. I've taken care of everything else.'

But Zola was serious that she didn't like to be surprised. She'd always been a planner – not knowing what was ahead made her feel vulnerable.

'Don't look so worried.' Mbali took Zola's hand and kissed it. 'This weekend I want you to leave all the worrying to me.'

'Then at least tell me where we are,' Zola pleaded. They were driving through an odd industrial area Zola had never been to before.

'We're leaving Midrand,' Mbali said. 'I took a few shortcuts to avoid traffic. Can you relax now?'

Zola looked around and still recognised nothing. 'So we're going to

Pretoria? And we'll be back tomorrow?'

'No and yes,' Mbali laughed. 'Just relax.'

Zola sat back and listened to the music, trying to focus on the lyrics of a song she couldn't make sense of.

Where were they going? Given that she'd had about five minutes to pack, she had hastily thrown a selection of things into a small bag, along with her toothbrush. Would her outfits work out?

Would she and Mbali work out?

Would her job work out?

And what about ... Rwanda? Seriously? *Rwanda?*

Why did Okuhle want her to go there?

It was all too much. In the warmth of the car, as the kilometres sped past, Zola felt her heavy eyes close.

When she opened her eyes the first thing she saw was a road sign.

Dullstroom 10km

'What's in Dullstroom?' Zola asked sleepily.

Mbali laughed. 'We are spending the night in Dullstroom. That's as far as my planning goes.'

Zola looked around still confused and Mbali squeezed her knee.

'I just want it to be you and me. Nowhere to rush off to, no one to bump into.'

Zola managed a small smile. 'I can get behind that.'

Mbali turned the car onto a small road that led into the bush, and as they crossed a gradual dip in the road, Zola was considering the possibility that they might be lost. But then it appeared: a small hotel nestled in the hills with a misty lake spread out in front of it. Mbali followed the bends of the dirt road until they were through the hotel gates.

A cold wind blew through Zola's T-shirt as she stepped out of the car, and Mbali draped his jacket over her shoulders without asking. She was so taken by the beauty of the boutique hotel that she felt sheer awe.

The limestone walls veined with flowering bougainvillea vines made her think of an old Romanesque church she'd seen somewhere before. They walked through the ornate wooden doors that were almost twice as high and definitely twice as wide as any door ever needed to be.

Inside, the hotel had all the warmth of a cosy home. The wallpaper and the paintings transported Zola to a time long before she was born, and she warmed herself by a generous fire while Mbali signed them in.

'I really hope I brought the right clothes,' Zola confessed as they walked down a carpeted passage to their room.

'Really? I don't even like the clothes on our backs right now.' Mbali snaked an arm around Zola's waist, pressing himself against her.

'You're too much,' Zola giggled. A shiver of anticipation ran through her body, and her heart thumped in her chest.

In their room, Zola was finally free to let the magnetic pull between her and Mbali take over, drawing them into a passionate kiss, their hands moving quickly, instinctively, over each other's bodies, caressing, undressing, stroking, feeling, and giving and taking pleasure.

Zola fell back into the feathery cushions of the bed, her arms reaching for Mbali's face, her fingers combing through the rough hair of his beard and running down to his broad rippling chest.

The cream white walls and the crystal chandelier above the bed swirled as Zola's vision blurred, her breath catching in her throat. She did not know where Mbali ended and she began as they moved as one.

Later, in the bathroom, Zola licked her lips. The bathroom was big – as big as her bedroom at home – with gleaming white porcelain features against the rustic pine trimmings and copper accents, luxurious and homely all at once.

In the shower, Zola stood under the jets of scalding hot water and let it wash over her body, relaxing her tight muscles. She had just allowed her thoughts to get lost in the steam when she felt Mbali's hand on her shoulder.

'I could stay here forever,' she whispered, leaning back into Mbali, allowing him to wrap himself around her as the hot water rained down on them both.

'I don't think I could do forever – in a few seconds we'll both be boiled.' Mbali laughed, wrapping Zola in a thick plush robe as they both stepped out of the steam. 'Besides, I've worked up quite an appetite. And I know the perfect place to enjoy it.'

Back in the bedroom, Zola crawled between the thick fluffy sheets onto the warmth of the bed and watched as Mbali pushed the room-service cart closer. It was heavy with an assortment of foods, fresh fruit, meat and cakes. Zola realised that she hadn't eaten all day.

'You really do think of everything, Mbali Thabethe.' Zola smiled, picking up a bunch of grapes.

Back in Jozi, Okuhle had spent much of her Saturday afternoon sitting across the table from a man with waist-length dreadlocks tied neatly into a ponytail behind his head.

'You're lying, I mean seriously, you're making this all up!' Okuhle squealed.

'I'm telling you, it was a nude hike hosted by naturalists,' Leruo said covering her hands with his over the table.

'In winter? Why would you do that in *winter*?' Okuhle asked between bursts of laughter.

Smiling, Leruo shrugged and leant back in his chair. He wasn't typically handsome – he didn't have any of the features Okuhle usually found attractive – but he made her laugh. And Okuhle felt as if she hadn't stopped laughing since she'd met him just the day before.

He was only a little bit taller than she was, his clothes were simple and well-worn. When he hugged her, all she could smell was sweat and fabric softener.

Okuhle looked down at Leruo's warm hands over hers, his fingers moving over her skin in circles. It was comforting – it soothed her. 'I should go with you on your next nude hike – see what it's all about since you insist it isn't just a bunch of perverts in the mountains.'

'Like I said, I did it once and I'll never do it again. But you're welcome to greet the sunrise with me any morning,' Leruo said with a twinkle in his eyes.

Okuhle giggled at the thought. 'I expected a little more romance before *that*,' she said firmly.

Leruo laughed, realising the implication of his innocent suggestion. 'Oh, I just mean that sunrise hikes can be *very* romantic. Starting with me ringing your gate bell to collect you at 5am.'

In the comfortable silence that followed, Okuhle blushed, raising her eyes to meet his every few seconds, and finding that every time she did so, he was staring back at her.

Chapter 29

An offer you can't refuse

Zola had had an amazing weekend, but even the cosy luxury she had experienced with Mbali hadn't been quite enough to make her forget Okuhle's left-field suggestion of Rwanda. Zola had wracked her brain and considered Okuhle's motives. As much as she and now her mother would want to keep Zola away from Mbali, surely neither of them would risk Larger Than Life by sending her all the way to Rwanda if they didn't think she was capable?

She dragged herself out of bed and slowly started getting ready for work, knowing she would be late, but deciding that she deserved some grace for all the evenings she had worked overtime getting ready for the expo.

'Zola, are you sick?' Nomsebenzi asked, stirring a pot of porridge on the stove.

'No, Ma, just tired,' Zola said sitting down heavily.

'Maybe you should call in sick,' Nomsebenzi suggested. 'You've been working so hard. I have the day off. We could sit and relax together.'

Zola sighed. 'I wish I could, but I can't let Okuhle down.'

Nomsebenzi shook her head with concern.

'I'm fine, Ma. I'll see you when I come back this evening.'

By the time Zola made it to the taxi rank the queue of people headed to Jozi stretched all the way outside the gates of the taxi rank. Women sat at tables of baked cakes and sandwiches, and sold amagwinya from buckets and tea and coffee in Styrofoam cups. They were women of her mother's age, and Zola could easily imagine them being part of her mother's burial society or women's group at church. Priscilla Msimanga was roughly the same age, but Zola couldn't imagine *her* alongside these women. Priscilla had said she and Zola were the same – but even if Priscilla had started out like Zola, there was nothing of that past left in her.

A convoy of taxis arrived and soon Zola was squeezed against a window she wouldn't dare open. As the taxi rattled forward, the thought of Priscilla passing change over her shoulder made Zola sigh.

Strangely, the ride to Jozi had become one of Zola's favourite times of the day. If she was lucky, she got to sit in the furthest seat on the middle bench of the taxi, and then she wouldn't need to get off until she reached her stop. This was her thinking time, and now she let her thoughts drift to Mbali, the weekend in Dullstroom, the feeling of his body on hers and how being close to him seemed to make her so reckless.

Thinking about him made her feel warm all over. Zola grinned as the taxi swerved into the emergency lane, passing the rows of cars stuck nose to tail in the morning traffic.

Her phone buzzed in her bag: Okuhle.

'Hey, Zola, how are you?'

Zola sighed louder than she should have. 'I'm fine, just stuck in a bit of traffic. I'm on my way though.'

Okuhle was quiet and Zola held on, waiting to hear why she had called. Her jaw tightened and her beaded tennis shoes felt tight around her feet.

THE THING WITH ZOLA

'Zola, please always call beforehand if you know you're running late,' Okuhle said in a cool professional tone that was new to Zola.

Zola suddenly missed the old Okuhle – the boss who so badly wanted to be liked.

'I'm sorry. I'll see you later then,' Zola said, hanging up.

She thought about it: it was unlike her not to call ahead, unlike her to have stayed over at Mbali's, unlike her to have lied repeatedly to her mother.

Was this what Mbali Thabethe had done to her?

For the first time, Zola arrived to a full office. She walked quickly to her desk and sat down.

'You look exhausted,' Khanyisa greeted her. 'I was jealous that you got to spend Friday at the expo but, geez, now I'm glad.'

Zola pulled out her compact mirror and looked herself over.

'It's just the bags under my eyes,' she argued. 'I didn't sleep very well.'

'Nightmares about that twins situation you had going with Okuhle? Because – yikes!' Khanyisa laughed.

'It wasn't that bad. People probably thought it was a uniform.'

Khanyisa pulled up one of the expo pictures she was busy archiving and showed it to Zola: it was of Zola and Okuhle standing in front of a banner smiling. Zola had never thought about it before, but she and Okuhle looked oddly similar.

'You did something to this picture,' Zola laughed, zooming in on their faces. 'We don't actually look so similar.'

Something in the corner of the photo caught Zola's eye. She had really wanted Mbali to be at the expo, but she'd known she couldn't ask him – yet there he was in the photo.

'Are these pictures in chronological order?' Zola asked, scanning through more of them.

Khanyisa nodded.

A few pictures later Zola noticed a picture of Okuhle wearing the same watch Mbali had taken back from her. It was so distinctive, she would have recognised it anywhere.

She felt her heart drop into her shoes. What was going on?

'Zola? Are you okay?'

Without a word, Zola pulled on her headset.

What a fool she'd been.

And it was not like she hadn't been warned.

For the rest of the morning, Zola felt broken. She really liked Mbali and she had desperately wanted Priscilla to be wrong about him, but the photos of him sneaking around to see Okuhle at the expo were proof enough. It seemed that everyone knew Mbali better than she did – and everyone knew he was a mistake.

'How could you risk so much for a stranger? No, sisi – choose yourself!' Khanyisa said out of nowhere.

'Excuse me?' Zola snapped off her headset.

Khanyisa's eyes were glued to her computer screen. 'What are you, Team Jayden? I really think Mellisa has a better chance with Syd. Even if they don't live happily ever after, at least they'll get the money.'

Zola was completely lost until she realised Khanyisa had an earbud in one ear and was catching up on a reality TV wedding show.

Khanyisa laughed as she saw Zola looking at her. 'If you tell Okuhle I watch *Surviving Marriage* at work, she'll kill me. Don't forget I'm your only friend in this office.'

As she turned back to her show, Zola wondered if there was a hidden message in what Khanyisa had just said.

I choose myself, she thought silently. Mbali could keep his fancy gestures – and he would not hear back from her again.

The offices of Larger Than Life may not have been redecorated yet, but towards the end of the week the reception area looked like a floristry workshop. At least one new bouquet had been delivered every day, amidst frequent deliveries of chocolates, jewellery, lunches and cakes. All were either for Zola or Okuhle, but while the messages for Okuhle were increasingly intimate, the messages for Zola were increasingly desperate. She still hadn't answered any of Mbali's calls.

On Thursday Zola arrived before Okuhle, which was the new normal, and discovered that there were bouquets waiting for them both. Zola took the flowers and put one vase on Okuhle's office, carrying the other back to her own desk.

'Is it the Romance Olympics?' Khanyisa asked taking a whiff. 'Is there a competition the rest of us don't know about? You should tell us so we can also join.'

But Zola felt uncomfortable. The gifts were too much. It had been just a few days since she'd decided to break up with Mbali, and he was already going out of his way to win her back – before she'd even figured out how to make the break.

As for Okuhle, Leruo had swept her off her feet and she was now too busy having an actual life to be interfering in Zola's life. These days she also rarely made it to work before ten o'clock.

'Leruo and I went hiking this morning – you should have seen the sunrise!' Okuhle gushed, coming into the office a short while later. 'We aimed for a quick five kilometres, but we got carried away. So we went the whole fifteen kays, and just enjoyed nature.'

Zola had thought Okuhle was a chakra hun from the beginning, but Leruo had somehow inspired her to step it up. This week's schedule had included yoga, meditation and multiple juice cleanses, which she'd constantly encouraged Zola to join her in. 'I swear, it will change your life,' she'd said about every single one of her new habits.

Okuhle didn't just sound different these days – she looked different too. Her hair had been plaited flat on her head and decorated with beads. Her clothes were simple and loose fitting: fewer florals and more paisleys, and high-heeled shoes were apparently no longer an option.

This morning when Okuhle went into her office she saw the bouquet on her desk, but when she dug through the flowers for the card, her heart dipped briefly. She carried the bouquet out to Zola.

'These are yours,' she said, smiling uncomfortably.

'Sorry,' Zola said, swapping the two vases and picking up the card addressed to her. It was a poem. While Mbali was making a serious effort with the romance, he definitely wasn't a poet:

My dream came true.
I used to be blue.
I didn't know love before I knew you.

Zola cringed; it probably wasn't the best thing for Okuhle to read, but Okuhle seemed sympathetic.

'It's okay. Really, Zola, it's okay.'

Zola believed her for once: all Okuhle's organic, freshly pressed pining appeared to be for Leruo these days.

'Anyway, can I see you in my office for a moment?'

Zola followed Okuhle to her office, and for the first time didn't feel angry or anxious about being there.

'So ...' Okuhle grinned. 'I have your new contract and those details about your new job. Starting with Rwanda, and then with Ghana, Nigeria and Botswana, we're going international with our corporate events division – and I want you to head Rwanda.'

Zola had almost forgotten Okuhle's strange proposal.

Okuhle squinted up from the paperwork on her desk. 'You look surprised. I know you're probably worried about your experience, but you'll have a really supportive team there with more than enough experience to cover you. You, on the other hand, bring expertise and an international perspective.'

Zola nodded taking in Okuhle's praises. It sounded legit, but how could she be sure this wasn't one of Okuhle's half-baked, half-mad ideas?

'Zola, you're nodding a lot, but what are you thinking?' Okuhle prodded, leaning back in her chair.

'It's a lot to think about,' Zola admitted. 'And yes, I did consider the fact that I have very little experience and this isn't exactly my field of study—'

'You're a natural,' Okuhle cut in. 'I know you can do it. You just need to believe it yourself. Say your affirmations.'

Zola held back from rolling her eyes. Next Okuhle would tell her to breathe through her stress. Okuhle was certainly giving her new lifestyle everything she had.

'I'll give it some thought and read through the paperwork,' Zola said thoughtfully.

It was Okuhle's turn to nod. 'Of course, it's a life-changing decision and I don't mean to rush you, but you'll see from the contract there is urgent business to be taken care of. It's a six-month contract. Very exciting.'

Zola took the envelope from Okuhle, her mind racing, and headed back to her desk. She sat there for a while with her chin resting on her palm.

'With a bouquet like that on your desk, I can't imagine you having anything to worry about,' Khanyisa said rolling her chair closer to Zola. 'Are these apology flowers?'

She reached past Zola to pluck a deep red dahlia from the vase.

'You know, Khanyisa, I sometimes don't know what you're talking about.'

The idea of moving to Rwanda still swirled in her mind. Of course she wanted to go – she'd wanted to leave home again from the moment she'd touched down in OR Tambo, so taking the job made sense. But things had changed since then.

She needed to talk to someone and the first person that entered her mind was Mbali. Even if she was mad with him, he might have the advice she could use right now.

Thanks for the flowers. Can I see you after work? Zola typed.

Seconds later her phone was ringing in her hand.

'You know you can text back,' Zola started.

'Then how would I hear your voice?' Mbali asked.

He had a way of rendering her speechless.

'Zola, I really want to see you, but this evening I'm meeting someone in Bassonia. But I can take you home,' Mbali said.

Despite herself, Zola's heart fluttered as she hung up. Sometimes Mbali ticked boxes she hadn't even known she wanted ticked.

Chapter 30

An anchor

'You don't think the timing of all this is strange?' Mbali asked. 'And that's being generous. Okuhle's mother really doesn't know when to stop.'

Mbali had offered to take her home – he'd made time for her, even if it was on his way to a meeting in the south. But the conversation was turning sour.

Zola sighed and leant back in her seat as Mbali navigated Jozi's bumper-to-bumper evening traffic. She watched cars struggle between lanes that were all moving equally slowly while taxis zipped along in the emergency lane. She never thought she'd be in a sports car wishing she was in a taxi, but it was happening.

'I don't understand why you've made this career opportunity about Okuhle and her mother,' she snapped without looking at him. 'I'm sharing an achievement with you, something I'm actually kind of happy about, and you've made it about your ex!'

It's not as if Zola hadn't considered it either but she sat, arms crossed over her chest, stewing.

Mbali blinked slowly as if trying to get his bearings. For him it was obvious: Okuhle had called in the big guns, her mother, to drive a wedge between him and Zola. He knew the job offer was more than just a coincidence, but he also knew what it sounded like.

'This is all still kind of complicated.' He sighed and turned the car into a tree-lined street that crossed a suburb. Rows of elegant houses with massive yards flew by on either side of them.

'Hmh,' Zola scoffed. 'Maybe it would be less complicated if you didn't sneak around visiting Okuhle behind my back.' She stared out of the window.

'What are you talking about? I haven't seen Okuhle behind your back.' Mbali clicked his tongue in a mixture of annoyance and confusion.

'The expo,' Zola said, pouting. 'I would have really appreciated your support that day, but instead you came to see Okuhle.'

'Zola, if you'd wanted to ask me about that, why didn't you just do it?' Mbali slowed down, even though there were no other cars around. 'Were you waiting for a moment to make the greatest impact?'

Zola suddenly felt ashamed of how the question had come out. She'd been angry and jealous when she'd seen the photo of Mbali at the expo, but deep down she knew his intentions weren't to hurt her.

He'd never done anything to hurt her. But somehow she had sabotaged herself.

She and Mbali had only been together for a few weeks. They should still be in the honeymoon phase, but here they were fighting about Okuhle.

'All I did was give her back her watch. I know what she was doing giving it to you …' Mbali winced. Somehow his efforts to keep Okuhle out of his relationship with Zola had put her right back into the centre of it. 'I should have told you. I'm sorry.'

Mbali's apology only embarrassed Zola more.

'Things are kind of weird. I got swept up in it and I'm sorry too. I don't know why I brought it up,' Zola said reaching for Mbali's hand on the gearstick.

Mbali pulled the car onto the freeway and picked up speed. Zola watched his face glow with excitement as he pushed down on the accelerator, his body buzzing with the thrill of speed.

'Maybe Rwanda wouldn't be such a bad idea,' Zola suggested. 'It would put space between me and Okuhle, and then you and I can build our relationship on our own terms ... What do you think?'

Of course she wasn't asking for permission, but Zola needed to know what he thought, where she stood, what would happen to this budding romance if she left.

'I already told you what I think,' Mbali said in a gentle voice.

It had been clear to him from the beginning that he couldn't tell her what to do, and it was one of the things he liked most about her.

Now it stood to hurt them both.

Pulling over outside her house, Zola expected Mbali to come in. He still had time before his meeting, but he was agitated.

'Greet Thobile and Ma for me. I have one more meeting for the day,' he said before speeding off.

Inside, Thobile was cooking in the kitchen and Nomsebenzi was sitting in the kitchen keeping her company. With two salaries, her mother's recipes had definitely improved. Today, Nomsebenzi had minced meat and colourful cubes of veggies simmering in one pot and bright-white rice steaming in another.

'Mbali says hi, but he couldn't come in – he has a late meeting today,' Zola announced.

She could already predict her mother's response, a slow nod and a comment about how hard Mbali worked. Nomsebenzi didn't need an excuse to compliment Mbali; she genuinely liked him.

'So, today Okuhle told me about an opportunity. I don't know all the details yet, but it looks like I'll be spending some time in Rwanda,' Zola said.

'Hmm, Rwanda,' her mother hummed, nodding. 'And you want to go?'

'*Of course* she wants to go, Ma,' Thobile said excitedly. 'We did an analysis of Rwanda's economic strategy last term – that place is happening. I can already see myself coming to visit you for the holidays!'

Once she'd heard a bit more about it, Nomsebenzi didn't need convincing either. 'At least this time you would still be in Africa,' she said, decisively. 'I agree with Thobile – this opportunity was meant for you.'

Chapter 31

Déjà vu

In her bed early on Friday morning, Zola thought about the contract Okuhle had given her. Signing it wasn't as simple as it had been the first time. Now Zola had things to consider, and something was holding her back.

'Zola?' Thobile appeared next to Zola's bed, comb in hand.

'Thobi, you scared me. I thought I was late. What's up?' Zola asked climbing out of bed.

'Can you do my hair?' Thobile asked pushing the comb into Zola's hand and sitting down on the small chair in front of the mirror.

'What is this about, sis?' Zola asked brushing Thobile's hair gently.

'Nothing. I just want you to do my hair and then we can walk to the taxi rank together.' It was clear to Zola that Thobile wasn't asking for the things she usually did. She didn't want money or clothes or fast food; she simply wanted her sister.

'When you went to Germany I was too young to actually realise what was happening. And now you're leaving again,' Thobile said looking up at Zola's reflection in the mirror. 'I'm excited for you, but I'll miss you.'

Zola sighed. All night she'd felt stuck.

'It's just six months then I'll be back,' Zola reasoned.

'But I'll be at varsity soon, Zola. Things will be different next year. I just want us to enjoy living in the same house while we still can, okay?'

Zola felt a sting in the bridge of her nose. Her eyes suddenly misted up and she knew that just one blink would send streams of tears flowing down her cheeks.

'I should get ready or we'll both be late,' she said, wiping her eyes with the back of her hand.

Zola washed herself quickly, her soapy washcloth flinging suds onto the wall behind her. With a towel wrapped around her she walked out of the bathroom to find her mother already dressed and making three cups of tea.

Nomsebenzi smiled. 'I thought we could eat amagwinya today so I woke up early to get them from that bakery on the main road. You used to really like them.'

Zola dabbed her eyes again and hurried back to the bedroom where she could be alone. What was happening? Her mother and sister had encouraged her to take the job in Rwanda – but now they were treating her like she was on death row.

'Mama, you're going overboard now,' Thobile whispered to her mother. 'You never buy those.'

'Hey maan, wena, Thobile.' Nomsebenzi flung up her hands. 'You complain when I *don't* do nice things; you complain when I *do* do nice things.'

Nomsebenzi focused on the kettle as if she could make it boil by sheer will. Something obviously wasn't right, and Thobile guessed it was the same thing she had felt since she'd gone to bed the previous night.

'You don't want Zola to leave,' Thobile said, laying their delicious oily breakfast out on three plates.

THE THING WITH ZOLA

'Did you hear me say that? Did I say I want to hold Zola back?' Nomsebenzi clicked her tongue and walked away into her bedroom.

Holding Zola back was the last thing she wanted to do. She of all people knew how bitter a person could become when they were stunted, and it was the last thing she wanted for either of her children. She wanted Zola to go, to see the world, to live a life exciting enough for the both of them.

But that didn't mean she wouldn't miss her feisty and determined eldest child.

Moments later, Zola walked into the kitchen with puffy, bloodshot eyes, sat down at the small table and stared at her plate. Nomsebenzi joined her two children.

Zola broke the silence. 'Mama, if you don't want me to go, I won't.'

Thobile looked from Nomsebenzi to Zola, waiting for someone to talk.

Nomsebenzi slurped her tea loudly and started to hum a hymn Zola and Thobile both thought was familiar but neither really knew.

'Personally, I don't think you should stay unless it's what you really want,' Thobile said not raising her eyes. 'I mean, you seemed excited about it yesterday. Zero regrets, sis.'

Under the table, she kicked her mother gently to prompt her to speak.

'What are you kicking me for, Thobile?' Nomsebenzi snapped.

The kitchen was quiet except for the sound of Thobile unnecessarily stirring her tea.

'Child, I will slap you,' Nomsebenzi threatened, slurping her tea again.

But Zola couldn't contain herself – she burst out laughing, almost spraying her tea across the room.

Confused, Nomsebenzi watched her daughter for a moment and then she and Thobile cracked up, and laughed until tears streamed from their eyes, until black eyeliner and mascara ran down Zola's cheeks.

'Oh my goodness,' Nomsebenzi said when she could form a sentence again. She reached out to hold both of her daughters' hands. 'I don't show it enough, but the two of you make me so happy. You've both already reached so much further than I did, and every time you do something new I'm excited and scared – but so very happy.' She took a sharp breath to quiet a burgeoning sob. 'I know how much you want to go, explore, challenge yourself, Zola. And if you tell me you aren't going to Rwanda, you'd better have a damned good reason.'

Zola sighed, and felt her anxiety leave her – until she glanced at her phone.

'Shit! We're late!' she squealed, leaping out of her seat.

'Zola! Not in my house!' Nomsebenzi shouted, rushing out of the kitchen too.

Zola had given up on taxis – she'd taken an Uber this morning, which had got her to work early despite her late start. When she arrived, there was no one there yet and nothing in the car park except for an unfamiliar rugged army-green Jeep.

She floated into the office buoyed by the laughter she'd shared with her mother and sister. Everything felt right with the world – and a decent conversation with Mbali would be the cherry on the cake. She was sure now that he had slept on it, he would see things her way: Okuhle wasn't just Mbali's ex, she was Zola's boss, and if Zola was going to continue working at Larger Than Life, she couldn't possibly be so suspicious of her motives.

Settling herself down in her chair, Zola took a breath as she dialled.

'Hey, babe. How are you?'

'Good morning, babe,' Mbali grunted his greeting into the phone. It sounded as if he was only just waking up. 'I wasn't planning on getting up for another two hours. How are you?'

'Great!' She hoped his grogginess wouldn't jeopardise the conversation she was preparing to start. 'So – I've decided to give Okuhle my answer today,' she started. 'I just wanted to know … um … The thing is, I've had to deal with miscommunication and disappointment in long-distance relationships, and I guess …'

Zola stuttered and stammered, hoping Mbali would catch on.

'I guess, I want to know what happens to *us* in these six months.' Zola felt instantly relieved. Now that it was said, the ball was in Mbali's court.

Mbali sighed deeply and Zola imagined him sitting up in his white sheets. She heard him swallow from his water bottle and clear his throat.

'Zola …' Mbali sounded thoughtful. 'I don't know how to tell you what you want to hear.' The strain in his voice was obvious. Instead of the deep manly boom he turned on for seduction, his voice seemed higher. 'I want to say the right thing, but I also don't want to lie to you. All I can do is respect whatever you decide to do.'

Zola shook her head, pressed her phone against her ear and walked back and forth behind her desk.

'It sounds to me like you don't really care what I do,' she said. Her shoes were hot and tight, and even though it wasn't even eight o'clock yet, her skin felt sticky and clammy.

'It's just that, Zola, I *know* these people. I know how they operate. As brilliant as you are, I really don't think that my ex and her mother want you in Rwanda just for your work ethic. Not now, just as we're getting to know each other,' Mbali explained in an even voice.

Zola felt the sting of tears in her eyes as the first of her colleagues filed into the office. She couldn't continue with this now. She wasn't going to cry in front of them.

'I'll talk to you later, Mbali,' she sniffed, and cut the call without waiting for his response. She couldn't imagine anything more he could say that she would want to hear.

As she stood up, Okuhle's office door opened and the smell of incense swirled into the rest of the office. Leruo walked out of Okuhle's office – Zola recognised him from the expo. He gave her a sympathetic look, then pressed his hands together as if in prayer and gave a shallow bow. Zola stared, surprised that anyone else had been in the office and unsure of the right response to a bow. Before she could decide, Leruo was walking away.

'Zola,' Okuhle called gently, 'can I talk to you?'

Zola walked into Okuhle's office.

'Leruo and I were just setting our intentions for the day when we overheard parts of your phone call,' Okuhle said plainly. 'Zola … I know what I'm talking about when I say this: don't put your life on hold for him.'

Zola nodded.

Whatever Mbali thought, she was going to Rwanda.

Chapter 32

Flying high

It had been a month of silent lifts home and awkward phone calls, and Zola would be leaving for Rwanda in just a few hours' time.

'You know, I would happily tell you to cut your losses and charge it to the game if I knew I would get my friend back,' Mthunzi said, taking a swig on his beer. Then he slammed the green bottle onto Mbali's desk and groaned. 'Even beer tastes bad with you around. This break-up is ruining my life!'

Mbali shook his head, refusing to entertain Mthunzi's antics.

'I've told you not to drink in here,' he said coolly.

Mthunzi walked out of the office swinging his beer in hand. 'It's not like I can even enjoy it – your mood is contaminating my beer! So can you please go to the airport and do that thing they do in the movies so I can have my life back?'

For the last month without Zola, Mbali had poured all his time into his work, with a little left over for gym and sleeping. Even his mother was worried.

'Are you eating, boy-boy?' Ongama had asked in a sing-song voice.

'Three meals a day, Mama,' he'd said dryly.

'Come home for a while. Your father isn't here,' she'd tempted.

'No, Ma. But thank you. I'm fine.'

He'd been touched that his mother wanted to help him nurse his broken heart – though he would first have to admit he had one, and he wasn't there yet. He was waiting for something to happen – something that would fix this whole situation.

Mbali looked around his office: at the worn old green carpet, the tired rickety desks. He smelt the acrid scent of Mthunzi's spilt beer. It was late already – it was time to call it a night.

As he dropped the blinds, Mbali looked down at the street below. Mthunzi was down there, talking through the open window of an old Jeep. The guy was a lunatic – what was he up to now?

Mbali pulled on his jacket and walked quickly down the stairs muttering to himself about how Mthunzi would get him killed one day. But once he saw who was in the Jeep, he knew he was more likely to be the one to kill Mthunzi.

'Okuhle,' he said grinding his teeth. His temple pulsed and he ran his hand over his bald head.

'Mbali. How are you?' Okuhle asked sincerely.

Mbali chuckled in disbelief and looked to the sky for a response.

'I see,' Okuhle said calmly. 'For what it's worth, Mbali, Zola seems pretty miserable too.'

'As if you cared. Why are you here, Okuhle? Are you here to be the shoulder for me to cry on? Pick up what's left?'

Okuhle winced. 'Actually, Leruo – my *boyfriend* – lives near here. I'm staying over so we can go to Bikram Yoga together in the morning,' Okuhle explained.

Mthunzi raised his arms. 'Biscof yoghurt? What? Why?' he slurred.

'Hot yoga,' Okuhle said, covering her face with her palms. 'Anyway,

I just went to drop off a care package for Zola. She's leaving for Kigali tonight. She's pretty cut up, you know.'

'I don't know why you're telling me this when you engineered the whole thing. This is what you wanted, isn't it?' Mbali exploded, pushing his hands into his pockets to stop himself from flapping about like a mad man.

Okuhle drew a few practised breaths. 'Is it absolutely impossible for you to imagine that I hired Zola because she's an asset to my company? You know what, Mbali?' she said as her voice lost its careful control. 'We really are done!' She wound up the Jeep's window and ground the gears as she lurched away.

'She's getting away!' Mthunzi shouted.

'I don't know how the fresh air got you even more drunk,' Mbali said dragging Mthunzi back into the building.

'Tequila.' Mthunzi laughed, pulling a mini bottle out of his pocket. 'But, seriously, m'fethu *Zola* is getting away. We need to stop her from getting on the plane!'

Zola trudged through the airport in the big coat her mother had bought her at the Oriental Plaza and the slippers her mother's manager swore stopped blood clots while flying.

'Cuz, who do we know in Rwanda again?' Zozo asked for the tenth time since they'd left Vosloo.

'No one, cuz, but if I think of anyone, I'll text you,' Zola said patiently and looked up just in time to see her mother wink.

She was trying to keep it together, but leaving was hard this time, even if she wouldn't be gone a year.

'It's unlike Mbali not to come and see you off,' Nomsebenzi said carefully. 'But never mind that. Relationships aren't everything. Take it from me – I've been single for more than sixteen years now and I'm *perfectly* happy.'

Thobile and Zozo shared wide stares that set Zola off giggling. No one believed Nomsebenzi was perfectly happy, but this was not the time to argue.

Zola led her family across the airport and got ready to say her goodbyes. She would be better off when she was waiting to board by herself.

'Zola!'

Her entire family turned to see where the voice was coming from.

A drunk man was running towards them, his body swaying so much it looked like he was about to fall over.

'Zola! Shtop! You mushtn't get on that plane!' the man shouted, and the whole airport seemed to grow quiet.

Nomsebenzi was the first to break the silence. 'Hey, get away, wena! Nonsense!' she said, waving her umbrella threateningly at him.

'Mthunzi! For heaven's sake! I can't take you anywhere,' Mbali gasped as he finally caught up.

Mthunzi took Zola's hands. 'We are here to shtop you from leaving,' he explained seriously, swaying on his feet.

'Never!' Nomsebenzi shouted, hitting Mthunzi's arms.

'No, Zola – we are not here to stop you,' Mbali said, struggling to catch his breath.

He had imagined having this conversation with just Zola but now he had her whole family watching, along with a few random strangers who'd been caught up in the drama.

'I'm just here ... Zola, I'm just here to tell you that I will call you every day, every *single* day until you come home,' Mbali said. 'And I want to see every picture you take, and I hope you take lots. I want you to tell me what you ate, who made you mad and what made you laugh. Everything! Because if I can't be with you, then I want to at least imagine that I am. And ... and I should have started by saying I'm sorry,' Mbali said, nodding at Zozo who nodded her approval back. '*Of course* you earned your promotion. You're smart and hardworking and I can't imagine anyone who deserves recognition more than you.'

Zola smiled, her eyes shining with tears.

'Okay,' she laughed. '*Now* you have my attention.'

Mbali wrapped his arms around her waist and without a second thought drew her in for a kiss to make up for all the kisses he had missed.

'Wait! Not while I'm here,' Nomsebenzi said, turning to look away.

'They're gone now,' Zola whispered as she fell into Mbali's arms.

'So ... is this going to be another long-distance relationship?' Thobile asked.

Zola nodded and Mbali grinned stupidly.

'Yes,' they both said together. 'Something like that.'

Acknowledgements

Gratitude does not begin to describe the overwhelming feeling I have for everyone who has carried me as I wrote this novel, but to name every single person who has pushed and pulled me through would be to write another book entirely.

I would like to thank my brother Ntuthuko; my mamkhulus, Anna and Nondlela; and my family for giving me the gift of time and allowing me to make this dream come true. My thanks to Nkosingphile and Siphosethu for reading my anxious texts; and to Sis'Tshidi, Kwazi and Neli for reminding me to take a break and laugh.

My friends Mamoshe and Vuyokazi listened to me ramble for hours about the relationships between people I had made up, and cared as if they were actual people.

My thanks to the team of busy people at Pan Macmillan for giving me this opportunity, for listening to and believing in my ideas. To Zodwa and Nicola for holding my hand through the various versions of this book and not letting me get carried away by my ideas.

I am above all thankful to everyone who takes their time to read what I have imagined, agonised over and written.